The Trials of Knights

The Heroes of Lotine:
Book One

This is my debut novel. I hope you enjoy and explore the rest of the books.

William Traverse

Copyright © 2021

All rights reserved.

ISBN: 9798324302283

This is my debut novel. I hope you enjoy and explore the rest of the books.

Ninos

For Mum and Dad
Thank you for supporting me throughout my writing journey.

The Trials of Knights

The Trials of Knights

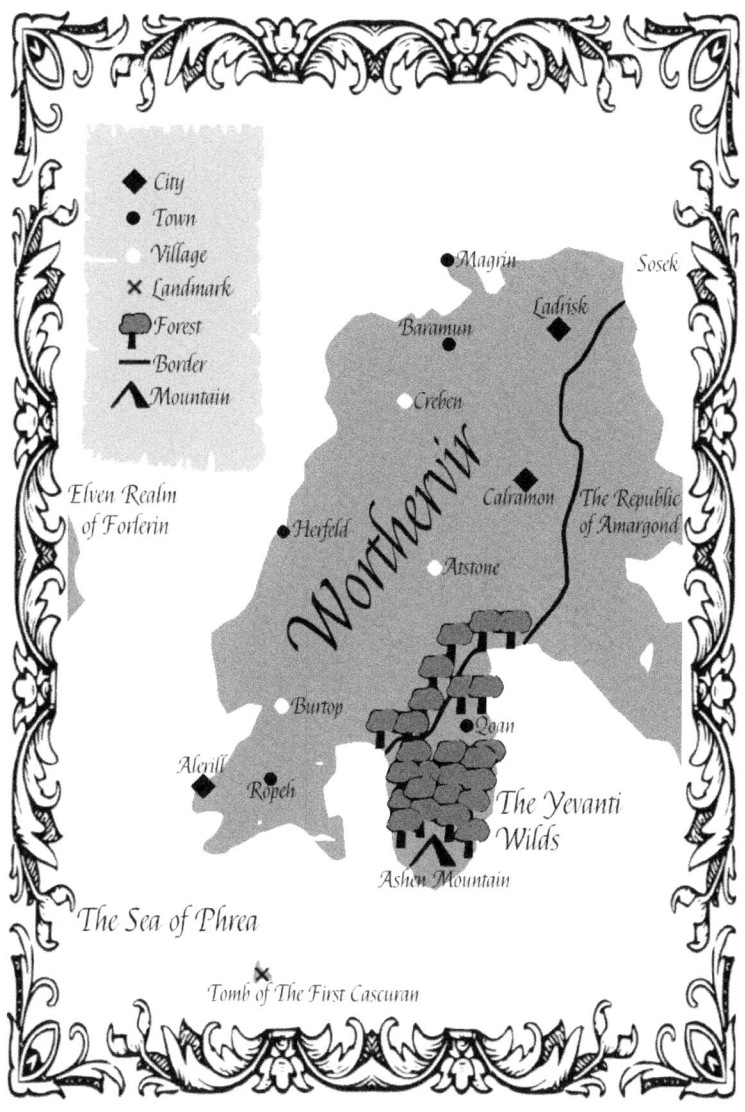

Part One

1

The village of Burtop was a half-day ride from the capital city, Alerill, of the country Worthervir. It had been home to Tarimev Riswaell ever since he was born. That was the day he lost his mother, and so he grew up being raised by his father, Cosai Riswaell.

Cosai spent most of his time, at least while Tarimev was young, tending to his farm just past the outskirts of the village. Tarimev formed a close bond with his father, but whilst Cosai worked the fields Tarimev would spend his time in the village, where he was treated like a son by almost everyone who lived there. All his life, he had nursed dreams of becoming a Soldier in the King's army. From a young age, Tarimev threw himself into swordplay practice with the village blacksmith, who was like an uncle to him, and the local scholar's teachings about the world. Once Tarimev turned thirteen, Cosai began to teach him how to run the farm. From that day on, Tarimev spent most mornings toiling under the hot sun in the fields. Unfortunately, shortly after turning fifteen, Tarimev's best friend, Imre, moved with his family away from Burtop. They went to the capital of the neighbouring nation, The Republic of Amargond, leaving Tarimev feeling lost. He spent even more time on the farm in a bid to have purpose.

It didn't take long for Tarimev to realise that the reason his father required help was that his health was beginning to fail. Cosai held on for a few years, but he eventually gave up his grip on life not long after Tarimev turned seventeen. With the loss of his father, Tarimev threw himself into the farm. He abandoned his dreams of becoming a soldier and spent his days trying to stay close to the memory of his father on the farm.

Four years passed, and Tarimev still remained at home, living a simple life and keeping to himself. His only company was the animals on the farm. But this changed when, one day, he was awoken earlier than usual by the sounds of screaming coming from the village. He jumped out of bed and threw open his curtains to see smoke rising from Burtop. He quickly grabbed his father's old sword and ran as fast as he could towards the commotion.

As he approached, he saw people running away from the village centre, carrying their belongings. He noticed the inn was aflame, and out the front, the blacksmith and innkeeper were engaged in a fight with three masked men. Tarimev immediately charged towards them, sword at the ready, and joined the fray.

The bandits quickly dispatched the innkeeper, and he fell to the floor, having been stabbed through the heart. The bandit that wasn't occupied by the blacksmith turned towards Tarimev as he ran towards the fight. He swung his blade down towards Tarimev, but he blocked it with his father's sword, sending sparks flying. He tried to counterattack, but the man easily dodged his attack. As the bandit slashed downwards towards his head, Tarimev stepped to the side, spun around in a single breath, and sliced the bandit's back from bottom to top.

At this same time, the blacksmith finished off both bandits he had been facing. He ran over to Tarimev and familiarly embraced him,

"Thank the gods you are ok," he said.

"What's going on, Marek?" Tarimev asked.

"They came out of nowhere, bandits who want our valuables and to take who they can as slaves. Anyone who can fight is trying to defend the place."

"Let's protect our village then!" Tarimev said with a combination of passion and fear.

The two men continued the fight alongside the other men of the village, but as the battle drew on, the bandits gained the upper hand. Within a few hours, all of Burtop's fighters were either dead or captured by the bandits. Marek and Tarimev were two of the lucky ones. They were tied up in the middle of the village, along with half a dozen others, as the bandits finished their raid.

The prisoners sat, contemplating what fate may befall them once the bandits finished the looting, but their pondering was cut short as Tarimev heard the sound of hooves getting louder and louder. Before long, the hooves were too loud for anyone to ignore, and as even the bandits looked around to find the source of the noise, a troop of a dozen King's knights came galloping down the main street. They had their swords in one hand, reins in the other, and with the visors of their helms down, they looked like a menacing opponent. The knights charged toward the village centre and quickly dismounted. Within moments, they had surrounded the prisoners in a protective circle. Two of the knights went to the centre and cut them all free of their binds. The bulk of the villagers stayed where they were, yet Tarimev leaped to his feet, grabbed his blade from the nearby weapons pile, and immediately joined the circle of knights.

As the bandits encroached upon the circle, the knights readied up for a fight, and the leader issued orders to his men. Tarimev, having no official training, ignored these commands and just got ready to battle. At last, the fight began, with the bandits charging toward the circle of soldiers and the circle expanding to meet their attackers. The clash of steel was deafening, but Tarimev managed to block it out and fight alongside the knights. It took mere moments for the King's men to finish dispatching a significant number of the bandits, and what few remained were now part of a desperate retreat.

Once the village was free of the threat, the Knight's leader approached Tarimev and said to him, "We appreciate your help. From what I've seen today, you could be a useful addition to the King's army. We are actually recruiting at the moment, if you are interested, come with us to Alerill and go to the training ground.

You can tell the Sergeant there that you have the recommendation of Sergeant Roskin."

Tarimev contemplated for a moment before replying, "Thank you, sir. But I have my farm to tend to. I couldn't abandon my father's legacy."

"Very well. Good luck in your future," Roskin said before helping his men tend to the wounded.

Tarimev made his way home, ready to be over with such a horrible day. As he approached his house, he discovered what other damage the bandits had done. His fields were nothing but embers, and his house was roaring with flames. He fell to his knees, distraught and in tears. Memories of all the happy times he had with his father raced through his head, and as he watched the roof collapse inward on his beloved childhood home, he felt like he could hear his father's voice on the wind, "Go. Follow your dreams."

He wiped the tears from his eyes and got to his feet as it dawned on him that there was nothing tying him down in Burtop. He dusted himself off, and with his sword in hand, he turned away from his burning home and made his way to fulfil his dreams.

2

After being given a spare horse by Sergeant Roskin, Tarimev spent the next four days riding and camping with the troop of knights as they finished their patrols of the area before returning to Alerill. Having never left Burtop before, when Tarimev saw the wooden gates of the capital towering in the distance, he realised just how small his world had been until now.

The ride continued towards the city, and as the group approached the gate, the Sergeant removed his helmet to identify himself to the guards stationed atop the battlement.

With a *thunk,* the gates were unlocked, and they slowly creaked open for the party to ride through.

Tarimev stopped for a moment to watch the bustling streets in awe, and he found it strange to see everybody walking around dealing with their own business. He thought about how, back home, you couldn't step foot out of a building without someone saying 'hello' to you.

Tarimev followed the troops through the streets of the capital until, eventually, the Sergeant brought his men to a stop in front of some stables near the centre of the city, just outside of the King's palace. Tarimev dismounted his horse as the Sergeant approached him and said, "Well, Mr Riswaell, this is where you leave us and return your horse. Only authorised people within the palace grounds, I am afraid."

"Thank you, sir," Tarimev replied. "How do I find the training ground from here?"

"Go back the way we came until you reach the square that we passed through, then turn left there and keep straight until you see the training courtyard ahead of you. Speak to Sergeant Koln, tell him I sent you, and he should sign you onto the recruit program straight away."

"Thank you, sir," Tarimev said as Sergeant Roskin turned away and began issuing orders to his men.

Tarimev began walking down the way he had been instructed, and before long, he arrived back in the market square he had passed through earlier. He began to properly observe what was going on around him, and it was at this point that he realised this city really wasn't anything like his village. Stood at this one point, he could see Elves, Dwarves, and Humans alike. All of them were going about their business, paying no mind to anyone that wasn't useful to whatever task was on their mind at that time. To Tarimev, this was a refreshing change of pace from everybody knowing everyone's business, and he realised that being away from Burtop would let him live his life without the constant scrutiny and judgment that came from living in a small village. Feeling refreshed from this thought, he continued following the directions that Sergeant Roskin gave him until he came to a courtyard surrounded by a metal fence. Within this courtyard were archery targets, fighting dummies, and even a duelling ring. Next to the fence was a large stone building, at least three stories tall, flying the flag of Worthervir atop its roof.

Tarimev entered the building and saw that it was almost empty, aside from some stairs to the side and a desk in the centre of the room. Sat behind the desk was an old man, youthful in the face, yet his white hair and battle scars spoke volumes. As Tarimev approached, he could see in better detail the claw marks that had scarred across the man's left eye, and with the milky colour of his iris when compared to his other bright blue eye, it was clear that the injury had impaired his vision. The man was hunched over his desk, writing something on the parchment in front of him, when Tarimev spoke, "Excuse me, I'm looking for a Sergeant Koln."

"You've found him," the man said in a gruff voice. "What do you want?"

"I was sent by Sergeant Roskin. He said if I spoke to you, I could join the King's knights."

"Well, excellent, we'll get you started right away. I plan to start training everyone tomorrow, and I happen to still be a man short. You should know, this is somewhat of an experiment. Usually, we would send recruits to train under a sergeant within a troop. This is the first time I have been asked to train an entire intake of recruits into a single troop. I reckon they just want to keep me out the way until I retire in two years, but you never know, it might work," Koln laughed at himself as he picked up a sealed parchment from his desk and handed it to Tarimev as he continued, "Take this letter to Grazan. He's the blacksmith in the Old Dock Ward, he'll provide you with a training armour kit. You'll need to arrange your own protection for your left arm though. We like that personal touch to follow you throughout your career. Welcome to the King's Army."

"Thank you, Sergeant," Tarimev said as he pocketed the letter before leaving the building.

Within such a large city, it was easy to get lost, which Tarimev did at least four times before finding his way to the old docks. Once he did, he saw they were in a sorry state after years of neglect. There were several ships moored at the dock, many of which looked to have been abandoned by their owners long ago. The buildings surrounding the docks were dilapidated and crumbling, and many of the windows were broken. Tarimev began his search for the blacksmith, but before long, he had to swallow his pride and ask for directions, so he approached a dockworker.

"Excuse me, I'm looking for a blacksmith named Grazan, do you know where I could find him?" he asked.

"Tha' tavern o'er there, The Sunken Maiden," the worker responded, pointing at a worn-down wooden tavern, sporting broken windows and a rotting roof, "I reckon 'e will be 'avin lunch there. Now get gone, I'm busy." He finished this sentence with an almost venomous tone, prompting Tarimev to make his way to the tavern without disturbing the worker any further. Tarimev entered, stepping over the door that had rotted off of its hinges at some point long before today, and approached the bar of the dimly lit tavern. The old woman running the place turned to him and said, "What can I get you, darling?"

"I'm looking for someone; do you know where -"

"You want to know something, buy a drink. Otherwise, get out," interrupted the woman.

"Fine, I'll have a mug of ale," Tarimev said as he threw two copper coins on the counter. The woman poured a mug of ale and handed it to Tarimev before asking him, "So, what is it that you need to know?"

"I'm trying to find the blacksmith, Grazan. I was told I would find him here."

"You were told right, he's in the backroom," she said, pointing towards a door in the back of the tavern, "I wouldn't trouble him at the moment though, he's in there with some people he owes money."

She turned to the pot on the fire behind her and began stirring it. Tarimev walked towards the door she had shown him. As he neared the door, he heard raised voices from behind it. He opened it just enough so that he could see into the room. He saw three men; two in blackened leather armour, their heads covered by hoods and their faces with cloth masks. The other man was sitting in a chair, his head pinned to the table by the masked men, preventing Tarimev from making out anything about him in the dim room. As he watched, he heard one of the masked men lean into the man on the table and snarl, "Last chance Grazan, where's our money?" He then punched Grazan in the

The Trials of Knights

jaw; eliciting a grunt of pain from him.

Tarimev stood for a moment, considering whether or not to help until the sound of a dagger being drawn from its sheath came from behind him. He froze as he felt the cold steel of a knife upon his throat, and heard a deep voice from behind growl into his ear "It doesn't look like you were invited to this meeting." The owner of the voice opened the door and shoved Tarimev inside, where he fell to his knees. He looked up to see one of the masked men walking towards him, who immediately grabbed him by the collar and lifted onto his feet. The man dragged Tarimev to the table and threw him into the chair opposite Grazan.

Grazan looked up, blood dripping from his mouth, and said "Stupid kid, look what's going to happen to you for being nosy."

"I wasn't being nosy," Tarimev said in a defensive tone, "I was trying to figure out a way to help you."

"Oh really, well that worked didn't it."

"*Shut it,*" one of the masked men shouted, as he hit both Grazan and Tarimev on the back of the head. Tarimev looked around at the three men and hoped to find an escape. While he contemplated this, one of the men started interrogating him. He pulled Tarimev's chair away from the table and stood in front of him. "Who sent you here?" he asked calmly. Tarimev looked into his masked face and said nothing, before being struck across the face by his interrogator. When he recovered from this impact, Tarimev threw himself up out of his chair, and with the full force of his body, rammed his shoulder into his opponent's gut. His enemy fell backwards and Tarimev seized this opportunity to leap to his feet and swing his fist at his other opponents. As the other two masked men approached Tarimev, Grazan also took his chances and stood up from his chair. He grabbed one of the masked men by the back of his hood and pulled him backwards with great force, straight off of his feet and onto the stone floor. There was a grisly *crack* as his head hit the floor, so Grazan left him there, blood pooling around his skull.

Tarimev was up against a wall, being pummelled by blows from both of the remaining men, and doing his best to curl up and protect his body. Grazan approached the enemies from behind, shoved the two men aside and pulled Tarimev back to his feet, "C'mon kid, stand your ground," he growled, "You take the little one, I'll take the big one."

He took up a fighting stance and squared up to the larger of the two men. Their opponents faced them and drew a dagger from behind their backs. Tarimev used this moment to draw his sword from his waist, quickly charging at the enemy he was facing. The enemy sliced upwards with his dagger, deflecting Tarimev's sword over his head, and then attempting a quick slice across Tarimev's gut. But Tarimev was prepared for this and was already swinging his sword down. He struck downwards into his enemy's shoulder with all of his strength before the blade came to a stop. His opponent fell to the floor so Tarimev turned to help Grazan, only to see him viciously smashing his opponent's head against the wall. For the first time, Tarimev got a proper look at this behemoth of a man, standing at least a foot taller and wider than most men. He was somehow made more intimidating by his long hair and beard being dyed a bright blue colour. Grazan let the body of his opponent drop to the floor before he wiped flecks of blood out of his beard, and turned to face Tarimev. "So, then kid, you must have a reason for wanting to rescue me. What is it?" he asked, "I haven't got money to reward you."

"My name is Tarimev Riswaell of Burtop, I am the newest recruit for the King's Army. Sergeant Koln sent me here for my armour."

"You got your letter of commission?"

Tarimev responded to this question by handing Grazan the letter he was given by Sergeant Koln. Grazan broke the seal and read the letter before continuing, "Okay kid, follow me to my shop, we'll get you kitted out."

Grazan led Tarimev out of the tavern and they walked to his shop without a word. Grazan opened the shop and ushered Tarimev inside. The building was run-down, with little stock on the shelves, and the majority of what was there was covered in rust. Grazan broke the silence and told Tarimev, "Wait here, I've got some recruit armour in the cellar. Take a look at my stock up here to pick your personal touch."

Grazan disappeared behind his counter, and Tarimev started looking at the armour pieces on display.

Eventually, he came across a set of decorated forearm guards; made from polished steel with black iron decorative swirls and a gold rivet on the back of the hand. They seemed to be the only pieces of armour that would hold up in a battle. Displayed next to them were a set of matching shoulder guards, from which Tarimev picked up one of each piece and put them on his left arm.

As he looked down at his arm to see how they looked, he heard, "My newest pieces they are, and they suit you," from Grazan as he re-emerged from behind the counter. In his hands was a package bound in fabric and string. He held it out to Tarimev, who took it without hesitation.

"Take the arm pieces as well," Grazan said with a smile, "They're a gift, a little something for helping me out with those money lenders. Don't know why I made it anyway, only business I get nowadays is making the knight armour, and even that is drying up."

Tarimev thanked Grazan as he took his armour and left the smith's shop. It took half as long for Tarimev to return to the barracks as it took him to leave. He walked through the front door and saw Sergeant Koln sitting at his desk. He looked up and said, "Ah, Mr Riswaell, you made it back. I was beginning to think you weren't returning. You took your time. Doesn't bode well, does it?"

"Sorry sir. Grazan needed my help," Tarimev explained.

"Well, in that case, you are forgiven, helping the people is the best thing you can do as a knight," Koln began, "Now then, I've assigned you a partner for your training. You should be able to meet him soon."

As he finished his sentence, a man entered the room wearing the same recruit armour Tarimev had just been given, yet he had on his left arm a golden pauldron, along with a golden gauntlet on his hand. He stood there with a smirk on his face and his hand on the pommel of his sword.

"Oh, excellent! You would have thought I planned

it," Koln laughed, "Tarimev Riswaell, meet Torvald Storheam, you two will be partners. Torvald will show you to your bunk, and I expect the two of you at basic training first thing tomorrow."

3

It was the break of dawn, and with it bells tolled throughout the city of Alerill to awaken the populace. Tarimev and Torvald rose from their bunks, along with the other recruits, to present themselves for morning inspection. Tarimev put on his new armour, which was nothing more than a chest plate, knee guards, and boots, all made of steel but nicely complemented by the shoulder guard and bracer he had chosen for his left arm. He joined the rest of the recruits as they filed out into the training yard and lined up in front of Sergeant Koln for inspection. Koln walked along the line of recruits, eyeing them up and down before checking their armour and weapons for anything out of order.

"You lot look good enough," he said. "I think you've got what it takes to make soldiers." He walked back to his place in front of all the men, then turned to face the recruits, and with a flourish of his hand, drew his sword from its scabbard. A few gasps were heard as everyone saw the weapon for the first time. It was a longsword, with an ornate blade decorated with golden runes etched into the metal. The hilt had been made to resemble the head of a bear, with a wide-open mouth. It looked like a weapon fit for a king.

"This is the blade I've used my entire career," Koln explained. "It has served me well over the years as it did my father in the Orcish war. But I'm afraid that to take it with me when I retire would be a waste, and since I have no sons to pass it onto, I will be giving it to one of you. Whichever one of you is deemed to be the best of this intake of recruits, will be given the honour of carrying this sword."

There was silence amongst the recruits as they all gazed upon the sword, and the old sergeant spoke again. "As you all know, you will be under my command for the next two years. Over these two years, you will be assigned various tasks to be performed alongside your training partners and eventually alone. You will also be required to perform the day-to-day duties of a knight. Once you are officially knighted by King Occime, you will be assigned to a new sergeant and placed within their troop. Throughout this program, I will be assessing you constantly until you undertake a final mission, similar to what you will face once you are knighted. This mission will be a test of all of your skills. It is at this point that I will determine who will have the honour of wielding my sword. Until then, I wish you all the best of luck. Just remember, I am here to teach you, so if you have any problems please come and see me. Once I have a task for you, I will send word. For now, patrol the city, and aid the citizens as best as you can. May Ajo smile upon you. Dismissed."

The recruits saluted Koln and set out into Alerill to begin their patrols. As they left the barracks, Torvald turned to Tarimev and said, "So, where do you want to start patrol?"

"I don't know," replied Tarimev. "Yesterday was my first time setting foot in this city, and even then, I only went to the old docks."

"That should be fun," smirked Torvald. "With how run-down that place is, I'm sure we'll find something interesting there."

Torvald led the way through the streets of Alerill, which were now bustling with people going about their daily lives. They passed the north market square, and the crowd of people buying and selling goods, as well as the stalls lining the walls of the town. They continued past the new port, where they saw the ships moored at the pier.

"Those are the merchant vessels," said Torvald. "They carry everything from foodstuffs to exotic spices from across the sea. The elves especially trade some wonderful foods, the dwarves not so much, unless you have an exceptionally strong stomach. If you ever need to get anything from one of the ships, make sure you have plenty of money. That stuff isn't cheap."

"I'll keep that in mind. What is there to do around here in our time off?"

"Well, I hear the taverns in the eastern end of the city are pretty good," said Torvald. "But I haven't been there myself. There's also the markets south of the city, but they're more of a tourist attraction. They sell all sorts of trinkets and curiosities, and some of the items are quite rare. You might like it since this is your first time in Alerill."

"You seem to know a lot about this city, did you grow up here?" asked Tarimev.

"No, I grew up in the City of Calramon," replied Torvald. "My parents were merchants, and they brought me to Alerill when they had attended events here. Only time I ever saw them was on official business if I'm honest. I almost became a Marçhal just to get away but I could never figure my way around magic. When I found out that the knights needed recruits, I decided to apply. It was either that or working with my father."

The two of them continued their walk across the city making idle chit-chat until the buildings started to become more dilapidated and the people wore less ornate clothes. "Well, we are definitely in the old dock wards now," Torvald said, "It's a shame what happened to this area. When I was a child, this was still being used alongside the new port to bring goods in. I think as the King put more money into his new port, he made it more difficult to use these independent docks. The final death knell was when the Shipwright moved his business to the port. Nowadays, the only people who dock here are those of an unscrupulous nature."

Tarimev looked at the old warehouses and shabby houses, wondering how many people lived in such squalid conditions. "Why does everyone live like this?"

"Oh, the rich people live on the north side of the city," replied Torvald. "Most of the nobles live in the Highscepter Ward. Any visitors to the city tend to stay in the south and the east. These people just can't afford to leave."

They walked along the docks and through the streets, passing the long-abandoned warehouses and rotting hulks of ships. The whole place had a desolate feel to it, like it was slowly dying. Eventually, Torvald said, "Let's grab some lunch. The taverns around here may be run-down, but they do know how to make a good stew."

Tarimev nodded his approval. "Sounds great."

Torvald led the way back until they reached The Sunken Maiden. "I came here yesterday when I was looking for Grazan. Caused a bit of trouble if I'm honest," Tarimev said.

"They don't give a shit about that around here," said Torvald. "If they turned away customers for causing trouble, they'd never serve anyone."

They entered the tavern and sat down at a table near the door. "Morning fellas," said the barmaid. She was tall and thin, with dark skin and short black hair. "What you 'aving?"

"Two bowls of stew please," replied Torvald. "And two mugs of ale."

"Right away," she replied and disappeared into the kitchen.

A few minutes later she returned with the drinks and food. "That'll be three Varre each," she said.

"Here you go," said Torvald, handing her the coins. "Thank you."

She quickly counted the money and gave him a nod

when she was sure it was correct. The two men thanked her then took a seat. As they sat and conversed, Tarimev noticed a man sitting alone at the other end of the room. He seemed to be staring intently at them.

"Do you see that man over there?" he asked Torvald, gesturing towards the man with his eyes.

"Yes, he's watching us," replied Torvald. "Any idea who he might be?"

"No, I've never seen him before."

Their food was delivered and whilst they ate, the man remained seated at the far end of the room, still staring at them.

"Maybe we should have a word with him," suggested Tarimev.

"Yeah, let's go and talk to him," agreed Torvald.

The two men stood up to speak to the stranger. When they stood, the man also rose from his seat and approached them. "Excuse me," he said. "I hope I'm not interrupting."

"Couldn't help but notice you watching us," replied Torvald. "Makes a man uneasy, being watched like that."

"Indeed, I meant no offence," replied the man. "My name is Hordo, and I was just curious if you would be able to help me. Are you knights?"

"We're knights in training," said Tarimev.

Hordo smiled. "Good enough. Could you help me please? These dreadful men, they've taken her."

"Taken who?" asked Torvald.

"My wife. She's been kidnapped." Hordo replied.

"Kidnapped? By whom?"

"By these thugs. Moneylenders they are, forcing

The Trials of Knights

people to take extortionate loans and then punishing them when they can't pay it back."

"How did they get your wife?" asked Tarimev.

"She was walking through the streets when they attacked and forced her into one of their wagons. I was right there and I just froze. I thought if I came here, I might find some mercenaries to help me."

"We will do what we can to find her. Don't worry." Torvald assured him, "Do you know where they might have taken her?"

"Not a clue. You could ask Grazan, I know that he has had trouble with these people in the past. He might know where they are based."

"Wait here, we will return this evening with news," Torvald said before wordlessly indicating for Tarimev to follow him. The two of them left the inn and Tarimev led the way to Grazan's shop.

Immediately upon their arrival at the Blacksmith's, there were clear signs of trouble. The windows were smashed, there was blood on the floor in the street, and the door was wide open. They entered the building and found Grazan slumped on the floor, leaning his back against the counter, a pool of blood and two bodies littered around him.

"Grazan!" Tarimev shouted, panic etched in his voice.

Grazan wearily raised his head and said, "It's all right, they're dead. I killed them both. Bastards came and tried to take me away, wanted to sell me into slavery."

"What happened?" asked Tarimev.

"They broke in and told me to come with them. I refused, they attacked. I managed to kill these two, but the other one ran off. He got me good before he did though." Grazan moved his apron to the side to reveal a deep wound below his heart.

"We need to get you to a healer," said Tarimev.

"Don't worry about me, I'll be fine." Grazan waved him away.

"Do you know where they would have taken you?" Torvald asked.

"They didn't say, but they've taken over the old shipwright's warehouse down where the city wall ends at the sea. I would guess that they are holding people there to put aboard a ship," as Grazan finished this sentence, he coughed, and a splutter of blood came out of his mouth onto his apron.

"Maybe I do need a healer," Grazan said with a laugh.

The two men carried Grazan outside. As they stepped into the street Torvald told Tarimev, "The Arcanists District is only a short walk from here. Let's get Grazan there then come back to deal with these moneylenders." Tarimev nodded and the three of them set off east, into the city and towards the arcanist district.

The three men made their way through the streets, which were now busy with people going about their daily lives. The sound of bells rang out from the temples, and the smell of food cooking drifted in the air. After ten minutes of walking, they arrived at a healer's shop, where they dragged a barely conscious Grazan onto a table and the healer began to tend to him.

"How long until he wakes up?" asked Torvald.

"An hour or so, probably longer if he keeps bleeding like that," replied the healer, "If he heals well enough, I will send him home later."

"Thank you," said Tarimev.

"You're welcome. If you want to stay and see how he gets on then feel free," said the healer.

"That's very kind of you," replied Tarimev, "but we have something to deal with." The two men turned and left the healer's shop. "I've been thinking about how much of a threat this gang is." Torvald said, his voice serious, "I've realized that we may need to get some help with this."

"Maybe we should."

"No, I mean we have to. If this is as big as it seems we aren't allowed to follow up without a Marçhal being involved."

Tarimev shook his head. "That's ridiculous. The knights can deal with this."

"It doesn't matter, it's the rules, part of the agreement between the Marçhal Order and the rest of the world. We should go back to the Sergeant and tell him about all this. He'll bring someone in."

4

Koln sat at his desk, deciding which assignments he could allocate to his recruits. As he sorted through the multiple sheets of parchment on his desk, the door of his office was thrown open by Torvald and Tarimev. They walked straight into Koln's office without knocking and began speaking at him. "Sergeant, we need your help with something urgently," said Torvald, standing before the desk.

"Excuse me, gentlemen. I do not recall you asking for permission to enter my office. Nor did I permit you to speak," Koln said in a very stern and loud voice, "Whether or not you are new to this service, you should still be aware of the basic levels of respect you should offer to anyone above your station."

Torvald and Tarimev looked at each other and then back at Koln. It was clear from their expressions that they were surprised by his tone of voice.

"Our apologies, sir," said Torvald, "but we have

discovered an issue that requires the intervention of a Marçhal."

"What is this about?" asked Koln. His tone changed to worry as he realised how serious this issue could be. The two recruits began explaining everything they had discovered about the moneylenders and the criminal activities they were involved in. After listening to them for a few minutes, Koln began to speak, "Gentlemen, what you have just told me seems very grave indeed. I am surprised no one has brought this up earlier. You are certainly right that this is a matter for the Marçhals." Koln pushed his chair away from his desk and stood up. "Come with me, we will go to the Palace immediately and speak to King Occime."

The three of them left the barracks and made their way through the city towards the palace. The palace was a large stone building, decorated with marble trim and stained-glass windows. The entrance was an ornately carved oak door with a knight on either side. The guards opened the doors for Sergeant Koln on sight and saluted as he passed by them. The three men walked inside and into the entrance hall. Koln led the way down a corridor that led to an open room with seating around the edges and a golden throne at the far end. The walls were adorned with banners featuring the crest of the nation, and the floors were covered by red carpets, the national colour of Worthervir.

King Occime Sunovren of Worthervir was seated in the throne. He was an older man, at least in his sixties, with pale skin. Yet he was still tall and imposing, with a broad chest and muscular arms. His greying brown hair was grown down to his shoulders and perfectly matched his short beard. He was wearing his regal attire of tan trousers; a blue doublet -the colour of the Sunovren Family- and a red cloak, matching the room's decoration. His crown was made of gold and silver and decorated with precious stones, as it sat proudly atop his head. He greeted them with a smile and waved for them to approach.

"Sergeant Koln, what makes you think you can come to my throne room without an invitation?" asked Occime. As he finished this question he broke into a grin and laughed, "How are you, Talbot? It's been too long?"

"King Occime, it is good to see you again," said Koln as he bowed. "It has been some time since we last spoke."

"Indeed, too long. I assume from the fact that you have recruits with you that this isn't a social visit?"

"No, not at all," said Koln "We have uncovered a very serious problem that requires your immediate attention."

Occime's face turned serious, and he gave Koln his full attention, "And what might that be?"

"Your Highness, there is a group of men in the city who are lending money to people who can't afford it. Then kidnapping them to trade them into slavery if they can't pay," Tarimev said as he stepped forward.

"What?!" Occime exclaimed, "Are you sure of this?"

"Yes, we have witnesses of it. We also know where they are keeping the slaves."

"Well, that is a very serious matter," said Occime "We need to take care of this immediately." The King motioned to a nearby guard and whispered something to him. The guard left the throne room and returned soon after, followed by an older looking elf in a surcoat, worn over armour which bore the crest of the Marçhal Order. His thinning, grey hair was braided down to his waist, with his facial hair neatly styled into a moustache the shape of a horseshoe. At his waist was a sword with an ornate silver hilt, styled like the rising wings of a bird, and in the centre was a bright blue gem.

"This is Marçhal Bergan. Tell him everything that you have discovered, and he will help you find the perpetrators of this crime," said Occime.

Koln and the recruits explained everything they knew to the Marçhal. Bergan listened carefully to every word they said and looked at them with a stern expression.

"I don't like the sound of this at all," said Bergan, "I want to get to the bottom of it as quickly as possible. Sergeant Koln, can you spare these men to come with me and shut down this criminal activity?"

"Of course," said Koln "These men are under your command for as long as you need them."

"Excellent," Bergan replied, "Thank you." He turned to the recruits and said "You two, follow me."

Koln watched as the recruits walked out of the throne room with the Marçhal and followed behind them.

The two recruits led Bergan to the warehouse Grazan had told them about. As they neared it, Tarimev noticed the sun beginning to low and realised just how long this first day as a knight had been, but it wasn't over yet. Outside the front of the warehouse stood two men, both in full leather armour with a longsword at their side. They stood next to the door, preventing anyone from entering or leaving. Bergan led the way up to the guards who saw him approaching,

"Halt. Turn back now or else," commanded the taller of the two men, as they both drew their swords.

"I am Bergan of the Marçhal Order, legal ambassador to the Kingdom of Worthervir. I'm here to shut down this operation."

"That won't be happening today, Marçhal," replied the shorter of the two men.

Bergan pulled his sword from its scabbard and pointed it at the shorter man. "If you do not stand aside, I will cut you down where you stand."

"I suggest you put that away before you get yourself killed," said the taller of the two men.

"You're wasting your time, Marçhal," said the shorter man. "It seems you have made your choice then," said Bergan and he swung his sword.

The short man ducked and rolled to the side, avoiding the blow. He got back up and charged with his sword. Before he could reach Bergan, Torvald had put himself between the two combatants. Tarimev had already engaged the taller man and they fought fiercely, but neither seemed to gain the upper hand. Finally, the taller man grabbed Tarimev by the neck and threw him to the ground. Tarimev's sword fell from his hand as the wind was knocked out of his lungs. He looked up to see his opponent preparing to drive his weapon down at him. Thinking quickly, he kicked out and swept the Moneylender's legs out from under him, sending him crashing to the ground. The two of them wrestled each other for a moment until the tall man was run through by Bergan, just as Tarimev was beginning to get overpowered by his foe. Bergan stepped over the body, helped Tarimev to his feet and handed him back his sword.

Torvald managed to knock the shorter man off balance and stab him in the leg, causing him to fall to one knee. He slashed his sword sideways and cut the man's throat, finishing him off.

"Good work," said Bergan, sheathing his sword.

They walked inside the warehouse to find that it was filled with cages, some holding people, others empty. In one cage, there were fourteen men and women chained together, unable to move. In the centre of the warehouse was an indoor dock, and waiting there was a large galleon, being readied for sail by a group of Moneylenders.

"It seems they've been busy," said Bergan as he looked around the warehouse.

"I don't understand how they have done this without anyone knowing," said Tarimev.

"We're in the Dock Ward, Tarimev. I would be willing to bet that we are the first soldiers to actually care about the people here for at least three years, ever since the new port was built," Torvald responded.

"Not the time for politics," said Bergan, "we need to deal with this gang before they spread further into the city."

"How are we going to do that?" Tarimev asked.

"We strike now, those who surrender will come with us in chains, those who don't will face our swords."

"Are you sure that is wise, Marçhal?" asked Torvald, "I'm certain they outnumber us."

"There is no other choice," said Bergan. "I'll lead the attack, you two stay behind me and wait for my order."

"Yes, sir," said Torvald and Tarimev in unison.

Bergan walked towards the dock and called out to the Moneylenders, "Surrender now, and you will live."

The Moneylenders turned around and one of them said, "It's pointless, Marçhal. We outnumber you and are more skilled than you. I suggest you leave us to our business."

"Evidently you have never faced a member of my order before," said Bergan, "If you fight, I will not hesitate to kill you. Surrender, and I promise you will not be harmed."

"Right then," said the Moneylender, a cocky grin spreading across his face "Try and kill us."

The Moneylenders charged at Bergan, but he was prepared. He stepped into the path of the first man and knocked him to the ground with a swift kick to the stomach. The second man rushed at Bergan, but he parried his attack and pushed him back. The third man charged, and met Bergan with a swing of his sword. Bergan moved his blade so that it was parallel to the ground and blocked the man's attack, forcing him to step back. "Recruits, give them hell," shouted Bergan.

The recruits did just that. They attacked the Moneylenders, swinging their swords with reckless abandon. But the Moneylenders defended themselves well and quickly overwhelmed the three men. They were slowly forced back until they had their backs to the wall and were surrounded by twenty men.

"Last chance, give up or die!" yelled Bergan. The

The Trials of Knights

Moneylenders burst into laughter.

"You're outnumbered and surrounded," said one of the Moneylenders, "what hope could you possibly have? The power of belief?" He finished his sentence with a mocking tone.

Wordlessly, Bergan stepped forward with his sword at the ready. He stood in front of his opponents, and the gem in his sword began to glow bright blue. His eyes changed colour to match the gem, and lightning slowly travelled down his blade. He extended his left hand forward and a burst of electricity shot out of his palm towards his enemies. The blast hit the lead Moneylender squarely in the chest, sending him flying backwards. The remaining Moneylenders charged Bergan, but he deflected the attacks easily and countered with a strike of his own. His blade struck the chest of one of his opponents and sent a surge of electricity through his body. The Moneylender fell to the ground, writhing in pain.

The remaining criminals continued their attack, so Torvald and Tarimev moved into a back-to-back position to hold off the enemies trying to flank them. At this same time, Bergan was cutting down enemies and blasting them with lightning. With the use of his magic, most of the Moneylenders were dead within minutes, and those that weren't had laid down their weapons. The Marçhal sheathed his weapon and the lightning surrounding him crackled away into nothing. His eyes faded back to normal and he addressed his allies. "Recruits, I have these men covered, would you free these prisoners?"

The recruits nodded and approached the cages. They unlocked the doors and released the people within. Most of the captives were bruised and malnourished, but none of them appeared to be seriously hurt. Once they were free and leaving the warehouse, the recruits helped Bergan move the criminals into the cages. As he locked the final door, Bergan turned back to the two recruits, "Well done," he said, "you've done a good job here. Keep watch of these criminals while I fetch some more guards to escort them to jail."

"Yes, sir," said Torvald and Tarimev, and they stood to attention.

The Marçhal left the building, leaving Tarimev and Torvald behind. The recruits stayed where they were, watching the prisoners as ordered. After half an hour, Bergan returned, along with a full troop of Knights who escorted the prisoners to jail. The recruits waited until they had all been taken away and then spoke to Bergan.

"Anything else, sir?" Tarimev asked.

"No. Thank you both for bringing this issue to my attention. I will brief the King in the morning and inform him of what happened here."

"Thank you, sir," Torvald saluted.

Tarimev and Torvald left the warehouse and returned to The Sunken Maiden. Inside, they saw Hordo sitting at a table with his wife.

"Sir Knights," he said when he saw the two men. He stood up and ran over to them. "Thank you so much! You saved her life."

Tarimev smiled. "It was nothing. Just our duty."

"We are indebted to you," Hordo said, his eyes filling with tears.

The Trials of Knights

"No debt necessary," said Torvald.

"My thanks again," said Hordo. "Please, at least sit with us and have some food."

"Thank you for the offer, but it has been a very long day. We only wish to get to our beds now, we just wanted to make sure you two had been reunited." Torvald said.

Hordo nodded. "I understand. Take care, rest well, and a final thank you from both of us." He shook both men's hands with great enthusiasm, then returned to his wife.

The recruits left the tavern and made their way back to the barracks. They arrived back around midnight and went straight to bed, exhausted from the events of that day.

Bergan woke early the next morning and ate a quick breakfast before going to see the King. He found Occime sitting on his throne, reading a scroll.

"Good morning, Your Majesty," said Bergan.

"Good morning to you too, Marçhal," said the King. "What brings you here so early in the morning?"

"I have news about last night's events."

"What kind of news?"

"The good kind. The Moneylenders were arrested, and the slaves were freed. However, it seems that the old dock wards are a hotbed of crime and poverty, and somehow it has escaped our notice."

"How is that? The Captain of the City Guard has never reported any issues with the area."

"We have many of the Moneylenders in jail. I plan to question some of them later and see if we can determine exactly how the destitute nature of the dock wards was hidden from us."

"Thank you, Bergan. Be sure to keep me updated with any further news."

Bergan bowed to the King before he made his way across the city to the jail. He entered a jail cell with an individual who had identified himself as a high-ranking member of the gang, and who had said he wanted to talk.

The Moneylender sat there, looking down at the floor so Bergan spoke first, "How did your gang hide yourselves from the city guard for as long as you did?"

The Moneylender looked up at Bergan, a look of shame upon his face that quickly morphed into a smirk before he opened his mouth.

"We didn't…"

5

It had been two days since the events at the warehouse and, for Tarimev and Torvald, they had been mostly uneventful. There were a few brawls here and there, but neither of them had any cause to draw their sword. Today they were on a break from city patrol, and they had decided to spend the morning in the training yard sparring with each other. They took turns attacking and defending, working through a series of exercises that would test their reflexes and endurance. The sun was high overhead by the time they were done.

"I think we're ready for lunch," said Tarimev, wiping sweat from his brow. "You want to go down to the tavern?"

Torvald nodded and they made their way back toward the gate. Before they arrived, they heard Koln shout from behind them, "Riswaell, Storheam. With me!"

The two of them turned around and saw Koln and three recruits walking towards the barracks. The recruits were wearing the same armour as Tarimev and Torvald, while Koln was dressed in full plate mail. He carried his bear-headed sword at his side as always. The two warriors walked up to Koln's side and saluted him.

"Good morning, sir," said Torvald.

Koln looked over at him and smiled. "It's good to see you two working so well together as partners. You are making excellent progress."

Tarimev nodded. "Thank you, sir."

"Now, come with me. Sergeant Roskin needs our help with a mission. There will be more details when we arrive at the palace. Let's get moving. We don't want to be late."

They followed Koln back toward the palace gates. When they arrived, they found the rest of the recruit troop waiting outside. All of them looked nervous, none fully aware of why they were there. Koln gave a quick nod to the recruits and led them inside.

They went straight to the throne room where Sergeant Roskin was waiting with all twelve men of his troop. He saw them enter and greeted them as everyone gathered around him.

"All right, listen up! The king has ordered us to form an arrest party. By now you will all have presumably heard about the Moneylenders that Recruits Riswaell and Storheam helped Marçhal Bergan shut down in the Docks Ward. Well, after some investigation Marçhal Bergan discovered that the Captain of the City Guard and the Sergeant of the Docks Ward Guard have been working with these criminals to hide the criminal nature of the district for their own purposes. Along with their men, they have been providing this gang of criminals with the means to terrorise an entire area of this city, and have even managed to hide the sufferings of the citizens from the King himself. As you would expect, King Occime is furious, and he has ordered us to bring in the Captain and Sergeant. Half of us will go for the Sergeant, the other half for the Captain."

He paused and looked around at the group. Everyone was stunned into silence, not sure what to say or do next.

"I know this may seem like a lot of work for one day, but we must avoid any tipoffs reaching either man. Sergeant Koln will take six recruits and six of my men to arrest the Sergeant of the Docks. I will take the rest to arrest the Captain. My men already know which objective they have been assigned," he looked directly at Koln, "Sergeant Koln, your roll call please."

Koln looked at the men. They were all expectantly looking back at him. He took out a roll of parchment from beneath his breastplate and read from it "Listen up recruits. Blaive, Ansfrid, Davit, Godelot, Raolin, and Charoth; with me. Hervonne, Ilbert, Riswaell, Storheam, Galter, and Balian; you are going with Sergeant Roskin."

The recruits all stood to attention and headed off to their respective groups.

Roskin led his group out of the palace and towards the Highscepter Ward, where the Captain of the City Guard lived whilst not in his rooms at the palace. At the Captain's house, they saw that several mercenaries were gathered outside. It seemed that the Captain had received word of their arrival.

One of the mercenaries stepped forward and addressed the soldiers, "The Captain isn't taking visitors at the moment. Be on your way."

Roskin stepped in front of his men and addressed the mercenaries, "We are here on orders of King Occime Sunovren of Worthervir, and we are entering this building. I would suggest you and your men step aside or face death."

The mercenary shrugged and said, "We have our orders and we have taken payment." He drew his sword before continuing, "You will not enter this building whilst we draw breath."

Roskin looked at the man for a few moments. "Then you will draw breath no more. We will fight our way through your men, and then we will take the Captain's house."

The mercenary smiled and said, "Do you really think you can beat us? You are only a dozen men against twenty of us."

Roskin raised his shield into a protective position with his sword at the ready. "I have fought men like you before, and I am still standing."

The mercenary laughed and said, "You haven't fought me. Let's see how you fare."

The mercenary moved forward with his men, and Roskin led his troop to meet them. The mercenaries attacked first, swinging their swords wildly at Roskin's group.

The knights rushed forwards, meeting their attackers with shields and weapons. Within seconds the first mercenary fell, his neck broken by a blow from a shield. A second mercenary fell shortly afterwards, impaled by a spear thrust.

Tarimev found himself face to face with a seasoned looking mercenary, who swung his sword at him. Tarimev parried the attack, striking back with his own sword and hitting the mercenary in the chest, but his sword deflected off the mercenary's chest armour and knocked Tarimev off-balance. Before he could recover, the mercenary kicked him in the stomach.

Tarimev fell onto his back as he struggled to regain his breath. He looked up and saw the mercenary's sword descending towards his head. Before it made contact, however, Torvald's blade cut through the air and stopped the mercenary's sword mere inches from its target. Tarimev kicked both of his feet up into the mercenary's groin, and he doubled over in pain.

Torvald stabbed his sword down and pierced the mercenary through his back. The mercenary's body went limp and his lifeless body slid down off of Torvald's blade. Tarimev began to get back to his feet when Torvald reached his hand out to him.

"Are you alright?"

Tarimev nodded, "Thanks."

He steadied himself on his feet and turned to face the remaining mercenaries.

"Keep pushing men! They're on their back foot," Roskin shouted.

The mercenaries hesitated, unsure whether to continue fighting or retreat. As the recruits battled, the Knights cut down mercenaries with ease. Soon, the last mercenary lay dead on the ground.

Sergeant Roskin stepped over the bodies on the ground and approached the front door of the Captain's house. He knocked once, and the door remained shut, with no sounds of movement inside. With one swift kick, the door flew open.

On the other side were three men, two of whom stood with swords drawn, while the third was the Captain, sitting at a desk with a goblet in his hand. Roskin entered the room and pointed his sword at his enemies, "Put your swords away. We killed your men outside, and we will kill you with even less effort."

The two mercenaries dropped their swords and stepped back with their hands in the air.

"Sergeant Roskin, I am surprised to see you here. When did you get back to the city?" The Captain asked.

Roskin ignored his question. "I have been sent by King Occime Sunovren to arrest you. Now come quietly, we don't want to have to hurt you."

The Captain stood from his chair and walked around the desk to stand in front of it. He looked at the Sergeant with derision, "You know that I cannot do that. I have held this position for near to a decade, I will not let you take it from me."

Roskin sighed and said, "You have been found out. I'm sure you realise that the King knows about your treason. If you come with us without a fight, you may face a more lenient sentence."

The Captain scoffed "A more lenient sentence? You are a fool, and you will pay for your stupidity." He quickly drew a dagger from behind him and lunged toward Roskin, but he blocked the knife with his shield and hit the Captain in the face with the pommel of his sword. The Captain fell backwards, painfully hitting the desk. Roskin pointed the tip of his blade at the Captain's throat and turned his head back towards his men, "Someone put this man in irons."

One of the Knights dragged the Captain to his feet, pulling his arms behind his back. Another walked over and removed some shackles from his belt before attaching them to the Captain's wrists.

The troop arrived at the palace with the Captain in chains. Two of the knights took the Captain into the dungeons and left him in a cell before re-joining the others in the war room, where everyone awaited Koln and his troop's return.

After a short time, Koln and his troop entered. The soldiers saluted Roskin as he approached Koln.

"The Sergeant has been arrested. He is awaiting trial in the dungeon," Koln stated.

"Good. Koln, we should report to the King. Recruits, return to your barracks. My men, you are to make your way to the Docks Wards and arrest the guards of the area in case they have any involvement in the crimes of their sergeant."

Torvald and Tarimev joined their fellow recruits to march back to the barracks, and Roskin and Koln made their way to the Throne Room, where they met with the King.

King Occime was seated on his throne, flanked by two of his guards when Koln and Roskin entered the room. Occime smiled when he saw them and greeted them in turn, "Talbot, Provel. I trust that you are here with good news?"

"Yes, Your Majesty," Roskin said with a bow, "We have successfully arrested both the Sergeant of the Dock Ward and the Captain of the City Guard. They are in the dungeons and my men are rounding up the rest of the guards that may be involved."

The King smiled again, "Excellent work, Provel. It seems we are short a Captain of the Guard, I would like you to take his place for the time being. Your men can serve as the guards of the Dock Wards as well."

Sergeant Roskin bowed his head and said, "Thank you, Your Majesty."

The King continued "Talbot, how did your recruits do with this task?"

Koln said, "They performed very well, Your Majesty. They followed their orders to the letter and had little difficulty making the arrests."

"Excellent, well I have some tasks for them. Relatively simple ones I believe, and I have already sent the details ahead to your desk. I wish you both the best and thank you for your service. You are dismissed."

The two men bowed to the King and left the Palace.

6

The next morning, Koln awoke early and began sorting through the missions he had been given for his recruits. He flicked through the parchments the King had left for him and eventually allocated each recruit a task.

One by one, he called the recruits in and gave them their tasks. Eventually, Tarimev was called in. The young man wore a nervous look as he entered the room.

"Riswaell," Koln said with a smile. "How are you this morning?"

"I'm fine, sir," Tarimev replied, bowing his head slightly.

"Good," Koln said. "I have your first mission for you. You're going to be escorting a merchant and a caravan of supplies from Alerill to the City of Calramon where you will take them to the mayor."

Tarimev's eyes widened. "Really? Do you think me ready to attempt this alone?"

Koln nodded in understanding. "No need to worry. You'll be accompanied by two experienced soldiers; Sergeant Roskin has agreed to spare two of his men. Knights Hirok Nentes and Alkin Domis, I believe you fought alongside them yesterday."

"Yes sir, I didn't meet them properly though."

"They are waiting for you at the port. Get your armour on, and meet them there."

Tarimev bowed once more and hurried out of the room.

Koln watched him leave, wondering if he'd made the right decision. Was he being too ambitious sending the boy out on such a mission so soon? But he knew that Tarimev had potential, and he had shown it tenfold over the past week.

Tarimev arrived at the port a short while later. It was bustling with activity, people running about and loading cargo onto ships. Tarimev walked down the dock towards the other two knights and saw that they were both wearing armour with the King's sigil. He felt slightly intimidated, but also proud to be trusted with a mission like this.

He stood in front of them, looking nervous.

"You must be Tarimev," one of the knights said. He had bright blond hair tied into a tight ponytail, and blue eyes. His face was angular and sharp, and he wore a brown jerkin with thick underclothes beneath. At his waist was a shortsword with a chain attached to the handle. "I'm Sir Nentes. Call me Hirok."

Tarimev shook his hand, then that of the other knight that he reasoned must be Alkin.

Alkin was tall and lean, and from his pointed ears,

Tarimev could tell that he was of elfish descent. He wore a chainmail shirt underneath a leather jerkin accentuated with the royal red of Worthervir, and had steel rapiers, with brass handles, on either side of his waist.

"Pleased to be working with you both," Tarimev said.

Hirok grinned. "Likewise. Now, let's get moving, looks like the caravan is almost ready to go."

They set off towards the waiting caravan at the end of the dock. Tarimev and Hirok mounted their horses while Alkin spoke to the Merchant they were to protect. Once all the goods had been loaded onto the carts, they headed off towards the city gates. Alkin rode in front of the Caravan whilst Hirok and Tarimev rode side by side at the rear.

It didn't take long to be out of Alerill, and once they had passed through the gates Hirok began to speak to Tarimev.

"Are you aware of why this mission may turn out to be extremely dangerous?"

Tarimev shook his head. "Bandits, I presume."

"No, we have to travel past the border of the Yevanti Wilds, and they are a violent tribe. They would rob merchants and caravans passing this way just for fun. If we are attacked, we may face some of the most deranged sights a man could dream of."

Tarimev thought back to his childhood, and the scary stories he and his friends would tell each other about the Yevanti.

"Do you think it will be that bad?"

Hirok shrugged. "If we're lucky, nothing will happen. But if the Yevanti decide to attack us, then I wouldn't expect to come back the same man you are now, if at all."

Tarimev shivered at the thought of being attacked by the Yevanti, but he tried not to show his fear. Instead, he smiled and tried to wear some confidence.

As they drew closer to the Wilds, Tarimev became increasingly nervous. What if the Yevanti attacked them? Would they be able to defend themselves? He wasn't sure that he was strong enough to fight off a group of savage warriors. He kept his eyes open, looking for any signs of danger, but saw none.

Eventually, they reached the edge of the forest that bordered the Wilds, and Hirok rode ahead to scout the area.

The sun was beginning to set when Hirok returned. "I found tracks. Nothing to say for certain it's Yevanti, but we should be cautious. I wouldn't recommend travelling at night."

Alkin listened to this advice and said, "We will camp here tonight. Recruit, you take the first watch. Anything suspicious, wake us up immediately."

Tarimev nodded, feeling somewhat relieved. At least he didn't have to rely on someone else warning him about an attack.

He sat on the ground and looked around at the stars above. The sky was clear, which made him feel uneasy, as if someone was watching him from afar. He looked at the others who were starting a fire, but they didn't seem to be worried at all.

A short while later, once the other men had set up tents and gone to sleep, Tarimev heard a noise from within the tree line of the forest.

He jumped to his feet and whispered loudly,

"Someone's coming!"

Everyone woke instantly, and they ran towards the sounds within the trees.

When they reached the edge of the forest, Tarimev saw a group of warriors armed with bows and swords. He could see seven men, all dressed in similar clothes.

"Yevanti. Back away slowly," Alkin ordered. "Don't make any sudden movements."

Tarimev did as he was told, but before he could get away, one of the Yevanti launched an arrow toward him. It flew through the air and hit him in the chest, glancing off his armour. He stumbled backwards, tripping over a tree root and falling. Before he could regain his balance and get back up, another arrow shot at him. This time it pierced his shoulder, and he fell to the ground again, hitting the back of his head against the floor.

He felt himself slipping into unconsciousness and soon blacked out completely.

Tarimev awoke to find himself tied up with his arms above his head. His head hurt, and he felt nauseous. He opened his eyes and saw he was in a tent, with the others. There was no sign of their attackers.

"What happened?" he asked.

"We were ambushed by a group of Yevanti warriors," Alkin replied.

"I don't think we were," Hirok said. "They were too organised, too militant. The Yevanti are fighters, but these men fought like soldiers. There is also the fact that we are alive, the Yevanti would have killed us, not taken us captive."

"Who are they?" Tarimev asked.

"No idea. But we need to get free of these binds and find out where we are."

Tarimev nodded, and looked around. He couldn't see any weapons, or anything useful. All he could see was a pile of dirty rags.

"Where are we?"

"They seem to have some kind of camp, don't know where we are exactly. They had us blindfolded." Alkin replied.

"How long have I been out?"

"Many hours, all of the night at least."

Tarimev looked at the entrance to the tent and saw sunlight through the gaps. He struggled against the ropes, trying to loosen them, but they were tied too tightly. He sighed and looked down at the floor.

"This isn't good," he muttered.

"Be patient, Tarimev. We will find a way out of this." Hirok said.

The three men continued trying to think of a way to escape this situation when the merchant, who they were supposed to guard, was dragged back into the room by one of the men who had attacked them. He dragged the man over to the empty post between Hirok and Alkin and tied him back up. With a sadistic smile on his face, he turned to face Tarimev and said, "You're next. You will come and speak to our leader, and if it doesn't go the way he wants, this will happen to you."

With that, the bandit drew a dagger from his belt and sliced open the merchant's throat. Blood spurted out, splattering across the floor. The man gurgled and gasped for air, but there was nothing he could do. His body went limp, and slumped forward, held up only by the ropes around his wrists. The bandit laughed and walked over to Tarimev, untying the ropes holding him up. Tarimev fell forward to his knees, his wrists still bound together. The bandit walked in front of Tarimev and grabbed him under his arms to lift him. As he lifted, Tarimev pushed up with his legs and headbutted the bandit in the stomach with all his might. The bandit doubled over, clutching his gut, and let go of Tarimev. Tarimev fell to the ground, and the bandit lunged at him with his dagger. Tarimev rolled to the side, and the blade narrowly missed his neck. The bandit cursed and lunged forward again. Tarimev kicked him in the knee, and a loud crack followed as his knee bent inwards and he fell to the floor.

Tarimev got up and rushed towards the dagger. He picked it up and leaped on top of the bandit, pinning him to the ground and stabbing the knife into the man's neck. The bandit gurgled a scream and writhed on the floor, but Tarimev kept stabbing until the man stopped moving.

"Nice moves, recruit," Alkin said. Tarimev thanked him and cut the ropes off the wrists of his two allies, and then passed the dagger to Alkin who cut Tarimev's binds for him. Tarimev rubbed his wrists and Alkin said "Well done, you saved us. Now let's go, we need to get our things and get out."

"Hold on, Alkin. Before we rush out there, I have a plan," Hirok said as he stood by the tent wall next to the entrance. "Stand behind me, and pass the dagger."

Alkin did as he was asked, and Tarimev joined the men up against the wall.

"Now stay quiet, and don't move," Hirok

whispered. "Help! I need some help in here!" He shouted.

A few moments later, two bandits stormed into the tent, swords drawn. They looked confused to see their former ally dead on the floor. Hirok seized this moment and stabbed the first bandit in the back of his shoulder. The bandit screamed in pain and stumbled forwards. Hirok released the dagger, whilst it was still in the man's back, and grabbed the sword out of his hand. He swung it at the second bandit, who parried the blow with his weapon.

Hirok ducked and thrust his blade into the bandit's stomach. The bandit gasped and dropped his sword, while Hirok followed up with another stab, piercing the man's heart. The bandit fell to the ground, and Hirok turned to face the first bandit.

"Come on then," he said, his voice cold and calm.

The bandit looked scared and hesitated. Hirok took advantage of this and stepped forward. He stabbed upwards with his sword, driving it under the bandit's ribcage and into his organs. The bandit groaned and fell to the ground. Hirok turned to look at Alkin and Tarimev, breathing heavily as he nodded at them. Alkin picked up the second sword from the floor, and Hirok passed the dagger to Tarimev.

"Let's go," Hirok said, indicating towards the exit of the tent.

7

Alkin, Tarimev and Hirok left the tent and found themselves on the outskirts of what looked like a small military camp. There were several tents and a few wagons parked around the area. A group of bandits, who were armed with spears, swords and shields, were training outside in formation.

"Definitely ex-military, we should be careful. Keep your weapons ready, and don't make any sudden movements." Alkin whispered, "Let's go. Follow me."

The three men made their way to one of the tents that was slightly set apart from the others. The door was open, so they entered cautiously, but there didn't seem to be anyone inside. Inside the tent were multiple storage crates, and off to the side was a pile of armour and weapons that the trio instantly recognised as their own. They quickly sorted through the equipment, found their articles and put them back on.

The Trials of Knights

"We need to get out of here," said Hirok, placing his hand on the hilt of his sword.

"Yes, but first let's see if we can find anything useful." Alkin rummaged through one of the boxes and pulled out a small bag filled with coins. "This could help. See what else is in here." Tarimev took this order and began opening more crates. Before long, he opened a crate full of flintlock pistols.

"Would these be any use?" asked Tarimev, holding up one of the pistols.

"For us, yes it will be. If any of these bandits have them then they'll be useless against us. Pistols like this fell out of favour for soldiers back in the Orcish Wars, seeing as they can't penetrate plate armour and they couldn't kill the majority of Orcs. Now you would only find a weapon like this in the Free Islands." Hirok said, looking at the pistol.

"So how do we use them? I mean, how does the gun work?" asked Tarimev as he placed the weapon in his belt.

"You load a ball into the barrel, and when you pull the trigger, it fires the bullet. It's not a complicated device, but they're hard to reload quickly." Hirok replied.

"I think we can handle that," said Tarimev. He picked up another pistol and handed it to Alkin. "Here."

Alkin nodded in thanks and placed the pistol into his belt. Tarimev grabbed another one and gave it to Hirok. The three men loaded their weapons and Alkin said, "We should get out of here, we don't want these men to find us in here."

"Agreed," said Hirok. The two men stood up and

The Trials of Knights

exited the tent. As soon as they stepped outside, the bandits training with their weapons were less than twenty feet from them. They noticed the movement from the tent and turned to look at the three men.

"Halt!" one of the bandits shouted.

Tarimev froze in place, unsure of his next move.

"Show me your hands!" the man ordered again.

"Get ready to fight, recruit," Alkin said, pulling out his sword.

"This'll be interesting," said Hirok, drawing his own weapon.

"If you say so," Tarimev drew his own sword and readied himself.

The bandits started towards them, each one with their weapons raised.

"Are you going to stand there all day, Hirok?" Alkin asked, clearly annoyed by his lack of action.

Hirok chuckled and threw his sword towards the bandits, and it embedded itself in the chest of one of them. He yanked on the chain attached to it, pulling it back towards him. He caught the sword by the handle and swung it around, hitting another bandit across the face. The blade cut through the man's cheek and he dropped to the ground, blood gushing from his mouth. Tarimev charged forward, swinging his sword at a bandit, who blocked the attack with his shield. He swung his sword down, aiming for the man's knee, but the man jumped back and avoided the attack.

"That's the spirit," said Alkin.

Tarimev struck the bandit again, this time cutting into his arm. The man screamed and fell to the ground, clutching his bleeding limb.

"Now that's more like it," said Alkin.

The Trials of Knights

The other bandits were now in disarray, and the three men attacked them mercilessly. The bandits fought well, but Hirok and Alkin were better trained and far more experienced. Tarimev did his fair share of fighting and had slain at least four of the men when there was a sudden shout of "Enough!"

The bandits stopped fighting and looked over at the sound of the voice. A tall, muscular man with a scarred face emerged from the crowd of bandits. The man walked over to the three knights and said "I apologise for my men. I am Yago, leader of this band of brigands."

"Well, you've certainly got some nerve showing yourself after what you just did," said Hirok.

Yago smiled and shrugged. "My men do what they need to in order to survive. I am sorry about your friend, but I can let the three of you escape his fate if you join us. We could do with men that have your tenacity, and you would want for nothing."

"How can we trust you?" asked Alkin.

"Trust is earned, I understand that. I cannot prove my honesty unless you give me chance to show you. If you are willing to join us, then we can leave this camp and move on to our next target. You will have everything you need; food, drink, shelter, and protection."

"You want us to leave the King's service and help you attack our countrymen?" Hirok snarled.

"I want you to help me defend my people, those that follow me. They would be no threat to you, nor would they pose any danger to your king. I would be grateful for any assistance you can offer."

Alkin looked at Tarimev and said, "Your choice,

recruit."

Tarimev didn't even think before he drew his pistol on Yago, and pulled the trigger. There was a loud bang and smoke billowed out of the barrel of the pistol. The bullet soared through the air towards Yago. It struck him square in the chest, tearing through his leather armour and straight into his flesh. Yago staggered backwards and fell to the ground, dead before he hit the dirt.

Alkin turned to Hirok and said, "What do you think? Do you trust him?"

Hirok looked at Yago's body and shook his head. The remaining bandits stood in shock, not sure what to do without their leader.

"Where is our caravan?" Alkin asked the stunned men.

One of the men pointed to a tent and said "It's behind there, we haven't even unloaded it yet. Take it and leave us be, we won't bother you again."

Alkin nodded and walked towards the tent the man had indicated. Hirok and Tarimev both followed him. Just as the bandit had said, behind the tent was the dead merchant's caravan. The horses were still attached to it and the knight's horses were tied up next to it. Alkin untied the Caravan's horses and climbed into the driver's seat, "Make sure you bring my horse with us," he said to Tarimev.

Tarimev nodded and untied both his horse and Alkin's. He tied the lead of Alkin's horse to the Caravan and mounted his own.

"Well then gentlemen, to Calramon," Alkin said, and he drove the caravan off.

The three men rode for the rest of the day and throughout the night. A few hours after dawn they crested a hill and finally saw the buildings of Calramon in the distance. They reached the city early that afternoon and made their way to the town hall. Alkin dismounted the caravan and said "Hirok, stay with the supplies. I'll take the recruit inside and speak to the mayor."

Hirok nodded, and Tarimev and Alkin made their way inside the building. They found the mayor in his office and introduced themselves. Alkin approached first as the mayor spoke to them, "Sir Domis, I would like to welcome you and your companions to Calramon. My name is Mayor Melden, I hope you find our city to your liking."

"Thank you for receiving us, Mayor. Your supplies are on a caravan outside."

"Thank you. Allow me a moment to sort the payment for Rifon."

Tarimev realised that this was the first time he had heard the merchant's name, and he started to think of the impact his death may have on his family, when Alkin said, "I'm afraid that won't be necessary. We were ambushed by bandits and he didn't make it. Please ensure his money makes it to his family."

Melden looked surprised and asked, "Bandits? Near my city? Where exactly?" Alkin gave the mayor the details, including the fact that they seemed like a military faction.

The mayor sighed. "Thank you for telling me, we had some soldiers disappear a month or two ago, I will send a troop to deal with them immediately. If you have some time to spare, I hope you can enjoy your

The Trials of Knights

stay in this city. If not, I wish you the best on your travels."

"That sounds fine, thank you. We shall rest here tonight, but we must leave for Alerill in the morning."

"Of course, Sir Domis. I am sorry about your troubles. I hope your journey home is more peaceful."

"Thank you, Mayor. May Ajo watch over you and your city."

The mayor bowed his head and said, "And may Ajo watch over you and yours."

Alkin and Tarimev left the town hall and headed back to the caravan. Hirok was sitting on his horse, waiting for the other two to return.

"How did it go?" Hirok asked.

"It's all sorted, we should find an inn for the night."

Hirok agreed and they made their way to the nearest inn. The three men spent the rest of the day enjoying drinks and talking with each other. As evening drew nearer, they retired to the rooms of the inn and enjoyed their rest.

The following morning, Tarimev was awoken from a deep slumber by Hirok, who was ready to leave for home. "I'm awake," Tarimev mumbled.

"Good, let's get going."

They packed their things and rode out of Calramon. They rode at full pace through the day and into the night. Midnight neared as they approached the gates of Alerill. The guards opened the gate for them and waved them through. They returned their horses to the city stables and Alkin said, "You did some excellent work over these past few days, Tarimev. I hope you will do just as well for the rest of your career."

Tarimev smiled and said, "Thank you, Sir Domis. I

shall strive to do so."

Alkin shook his hand and said, "I'm sure you will." Hirok finished removing his gear from his horse and said "You did good work Tarimev, I'd be happy to serve with you again." He too shook Tarimev's hand and walked away with Alkin.

Tarimev smiled, knowing his fellow soldiers thought well of him and made his way back to his barracks.

***

For two years, Tarimev continued with his training. He and Torvald both excelled in their roles as soldiers, guards, and negotiators. Everything they took part in, they were praised for. Over their time they learned more about the rules of the nation and the politics of the world. Their missions together gave them the chance to explore the whole of Worthervir and meet its people. The two became close friends and confidants to each other, and most people even mistook them for brothers. They often found themselves competing over who was better at a particular task or skill, but this did not stop them from working well together. In fact, it only made them work harder.

The King often assigned missions to Koln that he requested the two recruits worked on, including missions that put them in close contact with the Royal Family. Torvald especially was often working on missions that involved the King's daughter, Princess Cayte. It would have been hard for Occime to explain why he had taken favourites within a small group of recruits, but he could tell that they would be great assets to the Kingdom in the future.

Once the training program was coming to an end, Koln decided that it was time to give his recruits their final missions that, if they succeeded, would make them qualified knights, and allow them to take their title of 'Sir'. He reviewed how well they were all doing and decided which of them was worthy of receiving the first mission, and the honour of wielding his sword.

Part Two

8

Koln summoned Torvald into his office, and they sat in silence until Koln finally spoke up. "Torvald, I have to tell you that I am extremely proud of the soldier you have developed into. I have a request here from the King himself for your final trial. His daughter, Princess Cayte, is travelling to Herfeld for the opening ceremony of their Festival of Menobe, and he has asked that you are in charge of escorting her there. He has requested that Tarimev aid you in this as he believes the two of you are the best recruits we have, rivalling even some of the kingdom's best knights."

"I see," said Torvald, looking at Koln. "Thank you, sir, I appreciate the opportunity. I'll make sure she gets back safely."

"Good. Now go and get ready, initial preparations have been made and you leave within the hour." Torvald saluted his sergeant and left the office.

The day was bright and clear, and Torvald could tell that it would be hot. The air felt warm on his face as he walked through the training ground, where the rest of the recruits were doing their morning training.

"Morning everyone!" Torvald called out, waving as he passed by them.

"Good morning, Torvald," they all replied, giving him friendly smiles. He made his way to his room and changed into his armour. He exited the building back into the training yard and approached Tarimev. He explained the mission to Tarimev, who promptly congratulated him on his being selected. Torvald made sure Tarimev was aware that the King had asked for both of them by name, so he was not to be left behind. Tarimev gave him a quick salute with a smirk, and Torvald instructed him to follow him to the palace. They walked through the city, which was buzzing with excitement as preparations for the festival in Alerill began, and every settlement in the world that bordered the ocean was hosting their own festival to honour the god of the sea. People were busy setting up stalls, erecting tents, and putting finishing touches to their booths. It seemed like the whole city was getting ready to celebrate.

They arrived at the palace and entered through a side entrance, where they were led down a corridor until they reached an ornate door. A man stood waiting for them outside the room. He was dressed in plate armour adorned with the sigil of Worthervir and a cloak of the nation's colours. His face showed signs of age but his bushy eyebrows, jet-black muttonchops, and short stature hinted at him having Dwarf somewhere in his bloodline. He greeted them both with a warm smile.

"You must be Torvald and Tarimev," he said, extending his hand. "I am Sergeant Galeren, the Princess' personal guard. I understand you are in charge of this task Mr Storheam; I will bow to your orders during this time."

They both followed him into the room and took seats at one of the long tables. Before long, a beautiful woman came into the room, dressed in a royal blue dress that complemented her long, brown hair. Torvald and Tarimev had met her many times before and knew her to be Princess Cayte. She walked over to the table and greeted them.

"A pleasure to see you again, Torvald, and you too, Mr Riswaell." The two knights stood and bowed deeply to the princess.

"The pleasure is mine, Your Highness," said Torvald, bowing again.

She smiled at him and turned to Sergeant Galeren. "I am ready to depart, when do we leave?"

"That is up to Recruit Storheam," he said, turning to face him.

Torvald glanced at the princess; she was staring at him intently, almost as if she was trying to read his mind. He tried to look away but found himself unable to do so. "We can leave immediately if you wish, Your Highness."

"Yes please, let's get going," she replied, standing up.

Sergeant Galeren escorted her to the front door, and they were off, heading towards the stables. There was a carriage awaiting them there. "Galeren, would you drive? Myself and Tarimev will sit with the Princess," Torvald said with a commanding tone that he hadn't used before.

Galeren nodded and climbed into the driver's seat. The other three got in, and the carriage set off. Torvald and Tarimev sat next to each other, while Cayte sat across from them.

"I don't believe I've ever asked, how did you become a soldier, Torvald?" the princess inquired, breaking the silence.

"My father is a wealthy merchant, but I didn't want to join the family business. When I told him this, he got angry and disowned me for threatening his legacy. So, I moved to the capital and signed up."

"I see," she said, nodding her head. "What do you enjoy most about being a soldier?"

"It's the honour of serving the people, protecting them from those who would do them harm.''

"And you, Tarimev?" she asked.

"Ma'am," he replied.

"Why did you choose to be a soldier?"

"I have wanted to be a knight ever since I was a child, but when my father passed I had no choice but to take over his farm. Then, about two years ago, my village was attacked by bandits. A group of knights defended us and I saw first-hand how honourable these men are. Once I realised the bandits has destroyed my family farm, I knew I must join the army. I haven't regretted it since."

The journey continued for the rest of the day. When they passed through Tarimev's old hometown, Burtop, they decided to take a short moment to feed themselves and the horses. Torvald and Galeren took the Princess to the village tavern for a drink whilst Tarimev went to visit his old friend, the blacksmith. Tarimev entered the blacksmith's shop and greeted him. Marek looked up and smiled. "Tarimev! It's good to see you." he stepped out from behind the counter and embraced him. "How are you doing? What brings you here?"

"I'm on a mission for the King, and I thought I'd stop by and say hello. How are you, and your wife?"

"We're fine, thank you. We've been blessed with a child, healthy and happy. But enough about me, how is it serving as a knight?"

"It's hard work, but I'm learning every day." Before Tarimev finished this sentence, the door of the shop opened and a man wearing the armour of a Marçhal entered.

"I'm sorry to interrupt, but I need my sword sharpened," he said.

"Of course. Come in, sit down, I'll have it done before you know it," said the blacksmith.

"Thank you," said the man, sitting down at a nearby table. The blacksmith took the Marçhal's sword and left for the back room.

"How goes the travelling, Marçhal?" asked Tarimev.

"It's been a long day, but nothing too difficult," he replied. "I look forward to returning to the Citadel. It has been some time since I've been back there."

"You've been on duty then?"

"Yes, ambassador for the Cascuran Kingdom. I left Errinae Palace two weeks ago once my replacement arrived. Thankfully I have little to tell to the Order. There are more ships spotted in the Veiled Sea than normal but it is unlikely that it's anything more than pirates."

Tarimev raised an eyebrow. "Pirates?"

"Yes, the seas are rife with them, they raid all over the world, and the Pirate King seems to be more willing to attack major cities nowadays." Tarimev was about to respond when the blacksmith returned into the room and handed the Marçhal his sword.

"Thanks, my friend," said the Marçhal, as he handed a few Zela over and left the shop. Tarimev continued catching up with his old friend for some time before he left to return to his mission.

He returned to the carriage where Torvald, Galeren and the Princess were waiting for him. They travelled for another three hours until Torvald decided that they camp next to a small river for the night. He told Galeren to go ahead and make a fire whilst he and Tarimev assembled the tents.

Torvald and Tarimev pitched their shared tent and then the Princess' tent on the opposite side of the fire. Meanwhile, Galeren made a small fire and began preparing dinner. He sliced the meat and vegetables he had brought with them, added them to a pot of water, and boiled it. After this, he placed the pot onto a small fire, and soon the food was ready.

Galeren placed the food in dishes and handed it out to everyone. They ate in silence, the crackling fire punctuating the night. Soon after eating, the Princess decided to retire to her tent. As she stood up, Torvald said, "I am happy to take the first watch. Tarimev, I shall wake you in a few hours to take over."

"Thank you, Torvald, I shall feel safe with you watching over me. Goodnight." Cayte said. Galeren and Tarimev went to their tents and fell asleep quite soon.

Hours later, Torvald woke Tarimev to take over the watch, and went to sleep himself. Tarimev picked up his armour to put it on, in case of an attack, and left the tent to sit by the fire until morning. As he left the tent, he saw the lights in the Princess's tent flicker out. She must have fallen asleep without extinguishing them, he thought. He watched the flames dance and listened to the sounds of the forest around him. It was peaceful, he thought, and so quiet that he could hear his breathing.

Shortly after sunrise, Galeren and Torvald joined Tarimev by the now extinguished fire. The three men relit the fire, cooked breakfast, and discussed their plans for the day. Soon after, the Princess joined them, dressed in her usual blue dress. She said good morning to each of them, and Tarimev noticed a lingering look between her and Torvald. But he thought nothing of it and continued with his breakfast.

They packed up their belongings and got back on board the carriage. Tarimev volunteered to drive the carriage to allow Galeren to rest, who gratefully accepted yet still chose to sit up front, alongside Tarimev for the rest of the journey. They drove through the day and arrived on the outskirts of Herfeld Town around lunchtime. Tarimev stopped the carriage outside the town hall, and they all disembarked.

The town hall was a large building, built from stone and surrounded by a high wall. A wooden sign hung above the entrance that read 'Herfeld Town Hall'. A man wearing a long brown coat approached the carriage and greeted them.

"Good afternoon, travellers, welcome to Herfeld Town. I am the Mayor, please follow me inside."

"Thank you, sir," Torvald said as he shook his hand.

The mayor led them into the town hall, which was decorated with paintings of various historical figures. He showed them to their respective rooms and left for his duties. The three men helped carry the Princess's luggage to her room. She said "Thank you for your help. You may take some leave for the afternoon; the town guard will keep me safe in this building. If there is anything I need, I will send one of the guards to fetch you."

"Thank you, Princess," said Torvald. The three men left the room and Tarimev asked, "Well then, who fancies a drink?"

"That would be nice," said Galeren, "but I will rest in my room, I think. I will see you in the morning."

"Of course. Sleep well, sir."

Galeren turned and walked towards his room, leaving the two friends alone. Torvald and Tarimev exchanged looks, both thinking the same thing.

"We aren't on duty again until midday tomorrow," said Torvald, "Let's find somewhere with cheap ale and drink until we can't walk straight."

"Sounds like a plan to me," Tarimev smiled, "Let me get changed and I'll meet you outside shortly."

Ten minutes later, Tarimev left the town hall, no longer wearing his armour but was instead dressed in a cotton tunic and a shabby, brown coat. He saw Torvald waiting by the road, dressed similarly to himself but without the coat, and the two men set off into the town in search of a tavern.

9

From early afternoon till late evening, Tarimev and Torvald drank to their hearts' content. As evening drew in, the men of the town began piling into the tavern for their evening frivolity.

The place was packed with people drinking beer and eating meat from a spit. The smell of food made Tarimev's mouth water, and he ordered some roast pork. He had not eaten since morning and his stomach felt empty. It took him nearly an hour before he got to eat as many people wanted to be served first.

"I think I'm going to have to go on a diet," he said to Torvald after they finished eating.

"Rubbish, you're already skinny enough. You need to eat more if anything." Torvald said as he flexed his biceps.

Tarimev laughed. "You are probably right. Another ale?"

Torvald nodded and they continued drinking. They

were soon joined by a group of young men who sat at the other end of the table. They started talking about the latest news in the area. One of them said, "You 'eard about that ship seen nearby? Silver Eagle it's called apparently."

"What is so special about it?" asked another man.

"Come on, The Silver Eagle. How much more similar could that be to The Golden Phoenix?" said the first man.

"Oh yeah, because the Pirate King has renamed his ship and decided to visit Herfeld," laughed the first man.

The others laughed and Tarimev joined in.

"And how did you hear this news? Have you been spying on the Pirate King's ship?" said one of the men sitting across the table.

An old man turned around from the table behind them and said "I heard tell that the Pirate King has a favourite sailor, and rumour has it he had a ship made for him. I guess it is no surprise that the ship is called the Silver Eagle."

"I suppose that makes sense." said the first man.

"It does indeed."

"What else do you know about the Silver Eagle?" asked the second man.

"I don't know much, but it seems like a strange coincidence that they are nearby at the same time as the Princess is in town."

"That is true. The Princess must be here to see the Silver Eagle."

Torvald and Tarimev had both gotten intrigued by this conversation as it went on, and Tarimev asked "What would pirates be interested in the Princess for?"

The old man shrugged. "Who knows. They most likely want to kidnap her or ransom her back to the kingdom. Maybe they just want to meet the famous Princess of Worthervir." The men all laughed and the old man left the table.

Tarimev turned his back to the men and leaned towards Torvald, "Well that's interesting. Do you think they're here for the Princess?" he asked.

"I'm sure they are, and I bet we will find out soon enough. That is tomorrow's problem though, tonight we should have fun."

Tarimev laughed and downed the rest of his ale. He stood up and ordered another round of drinks.

As midnight drew closer, both men were extremely drunk. They staggered out of the tavern and into the night air. The streets were full of drunken revellers making their way home.

They walked through the streets laughing loudly and singing songs. The state that they were in meant they couldn't remember the way back to the Town Hall. They wandered aimlessly through the town, in hope of finding it, to no avail.

After walking for nearly an hour, they finally came across another tavern, but they didn't even realise it was the same one they had been in earlier. They made funny drunken noises as they stumbled inside and ordered more drinks. They sat down next to each other and laughed at their foolishness.

They decided that they needed sleep, but still unsure of how to return to their lodgings, they each rented a room in the tavern and made their way upstairs.

The Trials of Knights

Tarimev lay on his bed and stared up at the ceiling. His head was spinning and he felt like he was going to throw up. He stood to remove his tunic and fell backwards onto the bed. He passed out almost instantly.

Tarimev awoke with a start. He looked around the room. The sun was shining in through a crack in the window, and he could hear the sound of laughter coming from outside.

He climbed off the bed and walked over to the window. He pulled open the shutters and let the warm sunlight fill the room.

His stomach rumbled and he realised that he hadn't eaten anything since last night. He picked up his tunic and pulled it over his head before making his way downstairs.

The tavern was bustling with the workers of the town enjoying their breakfasts. Tarimev wandered over to the bar and ordered some bread and cheese. As he waited for his breakfast, he thought about the previous night. He remembered drinking far too much and hoped he hadn't embarrassed himself in front of Torvald. He had just taken a seat at the bar when he heard a loud whistle. Turning round, he saw Torvald sitting at a table and beckoning him over.

"Morning, Torvald," Tarimev said as he took a seat opposite his friend.

"Good morning to you, my friend. Did you sleep well?"

"If you can call unconsciousness sleep."

"I was there myself. How is your head? Mine is killing me," Torvald laughed.

"It feels fine now, but I don't think I'll ever drink again."

"I wouldn't worry about it too much. We are both young and strong, we will recover." As Torvald finished this sentence, the barmaid approached the table with two plates in her hands. She placed them on the table and left without saying a word.

"Finally. I hope you don't mind, I ordered us some breakfast," Torvald asked as he began eating.

Tarimev looked down at his plate and saw three eggs, four sausages and a hunk of bread. "I only ordered some bread and cheese. This will do much better than that," he replied.

"You need something in your stomach after all that alcohol. Now, onto business. Seeing as the princess is giving her speech at the docks, I think there is a very real chance that the pirates will attack there. Any attack will come during the speech, most likely near the end as we are more likely to let our guard down thinking any danger has passed."

"Hmm, you might be right. How many men should we have at the docks in preparation?"

"We should have half the town guard, which should be about ten men, ready to go. But I think you and I need to blend in the crowd, make it less obvious that we are there. Galeren can be on stage with the Princess."

"So, what do you suggest?"

"I want you to get some clothes from the tailor down the road, and see if you can get some more mercantile looking weapons from the blacksmith. I'm thinking rapiers?"

Tarimev stroked his newly-grown beard as he

thought about what Torvald had suggested. "That sounds like a good plan, I'll see what I can do."

"Meet me at the Town Hall at noon so we can change. I will inform everyone involved about our plan in the meantime, and take this." Torvald handed a sack of coins to Tarimev who took a look inside. In the bag was a variety of coins, from the lowest value of the realm, the Varre, up through the Sudra and Zela, and there was even some of the extremely valuable Linya coins.

"There must be at least ten Linya in here," he said in a shocked but hushed tone.

"Just over thirteen."

"Are you sure about this? This could almost buy a house in the Highscepter Ward."

"Absolutely. I know you'll bring back what you don't spend."

"You're very trusting," Tarimev said, with a small chuckle, as he ate his last bite of sausage and stood up from the table.

Tarimev left the tavern and made his way towards the tailor's shop that Torvald had mentioned. He entered the small building and went to the counter, where the tailor was busy working.

"Yes?" The man asked as he looked up from his work.

"I'm looking to buy some clothes befitting of a merchant. Two different outfits," Tarimev said politely.

"I know just the items, please wait here a moment," the tailor replied.

He disappeared into the back room and returned

shortly with two doublets, one blue and one brown; a long light brown coat; a blue wide-brimmed hat with a red feather in it; and two pairs of buckled shoes. "These look to be about your size. Will these do?"

"Yes, they will do nicely."

The tailor smiled and packed up the items. "Thank you for your patronage, I hope to see you again," he said as he handed the items to Tarimev.

"Thank you," Tarimev replied, giving a handful of coins to the tailor.

He left the shop and made his way towards the blacksmith. It was smaller than the tailor's, but still large enough to house an anvil, forge, and various other tools. He entered the shop and looked around for someone to help him. There were several people in the shop perusing the wares. Tarimev walked up to a tall man wearing a leather apron. "Excuse me, I presume you are the blacksmith?"

The man turned to face Tarimev and he could see that his hair was shaved at the sides and combed over the top of his head. His face was covered in scars, with a thick beard covering his chin. "I am. What you after?"

"I'm looking for some swords. Two rapiers, if possible," he replied.

The blacksmith nodded. "Certainly, that won't be a problem. Let me show you what I have available." He led Tarimev through the shop to a display of weapons. On the wall behind it hung a variety of blades, some of which were obviously decorative, while others looked more functional.

"Here we are, this is what I have available. Do you know what type of blade you would prefer?"

"Something stylish, but functional. Most importantly, cheap."

"Everything I make is functional, but these are the cheapest I have," he said, and he picked up two of the blades from the display to show Tarimev.

"They're not bad, but they aren't exactly fashionable," Tarimev said as he examined the blades. The blacksmith laughed, "You won't get cheap and fashionable in the same sword."

"Fair point," Tarimev replied. "I'll take them both."

"With weapons like this I guess you're off to sea. You might want some pistols as well."

"I already have one, just the swords, thanks."

"Very well. That'll be thirty Sudra then."

Tarimev pulled out the coins from his pouch and gave them to the blacksmith. He took the money and handed the blades over. "If you need anything else, come back to my shop."

"Thank you," Tarimev said before he left.

He walked down the street and headed towards the Town Hall. As he walked, he could see that the streets were full of people milling about, preparing for the festivities that were to take place over the next few days. He saw many merchants selling their wares from stalls along the road. Tarimev's eyes wandered from stall to stall as he looked at the goods being sold. He passed by a man selling barrels of ale, another selling trinkets, and another selling tanned hides. He continued towards the town hall, arriving an hour before he was due to meet Torvald.

He walked inside and went to his room to change; he chose to wear the blue doublet and hat and attached a rapier to his belt. He checked himself in the mirror and adjusted his hair, making sure it was neatly groomed. He picked up the brown coat and doublet and walked downstairs to join Torvald in the main hall.

Torvald was waiting for him when he entered the hall. "Well, how do I look?"

"Good enough," Torvald replied. "You've got my clothes?"

"Here you go," Tarimev said as he handed Torvald his disguise.

"Thanks," Torvald said before he changed into the clothes. "Let's get going, everyone else is in position."

They walked out of the town hall and began the short walk to the docks where the Festival of Menobe was being opened by Princess Cayte.

10

When the sun reached its noon peak, Tarimev and Torvald were already hidden amongst the crowd of people who had gathered to see the Princess's speech. On the stage was a row of dignitaries there for the proceedings, and on the end was Princess Cayte, with Sergeant Galeren standing behind her. Tarimev and Torvald watched as the Mayor of Herfeld spoke about the festivities and explained what events would be taking place. In his final sentence he handed over to the princess.

"It is my pleasure to introduce you all to our beloved Princess Cayte, daughter of King Occime Sunovren and Queen Lorea." The crowd applauded loudly as she walked up onto the stage. "Princess Cayte will now give us a short speech on behalf of her father."

Cayte stood at the front of the stage with her hands

clasped together, her head bowed low. As she opened her mouth to begin there was a sudden scream from the side of the stage. The crowd fell silent when one of the city guards fall to the ground, dead, with a man in a long, black coat and a tricorn standing over him holding a cutlass.

"Princess, run!" Torvald cried, pushing his way through the crowd. Tarimev followed him as Cayte turned around and ran off stage. The other guard at the side of the stage started to raise his sword; but before he could bring it down, two armed men emerged from the crowd. One of them ran the guard through with his sword and let his body drop.

Torvald turned to Tarimev and said, "I'll go after the Princess. You help the guards hold them off."

Tarimev nodded and drew his sword from its scabbard. He ran around the stage, in pursuit of the man in the long coat. The man had started to give chase to the Princess, but Tarimev was upon him before he had the chance to get to her. The man tried to swing his sword at Tarimev but he parried the attack. He thrust his sword towards the man's chest, but he quickly ducked under the attack and pushed Tarimev back. The man lunged forward and grabbed Tarimev by the neck, before slamming him to the ground and kicking him in the ribs. He went to kick again but Tarimev rolled to the side and managed to grab the man's leg. He pulled hard on the man's ankle and made him lose his balance.

The man stumbled backwards and tripped over the fallen guard. He fell heavily onto his back, his legs bouncing into the air. Tarimev took this opportunity to clamber to his feet and take up his fighting stance again. Before his opponent managed to stand, another man in the clothing of a sailor stepped in front of Tarimev and raised his sword to match him.

"I've got your back, Cap'n," said the man in front of Tarimev. Now that he was faced with two enemy combatants, Tarimev froze in worry for a moment, giving the man on the ground the opportunity to clamber to his feet and raise his sword. For the first time, Tarimev got a good look at his foe. He was young, less than a decade older than Tarimev, with scruffy, blonde hair down to his shoulders and mutton chops joined by a moustache, all dirtied by the grime of the sea. The captain glanced at his man before looking right back to Tarimev. He ran forward and slashed his sword at Tarimev's face, who stepped to the side and used the tip of his rapier to deflect the cutlass away from him.

Tarimev's footwork had placed him squarely in front of the second man who now went to stab his sword into Tarimev's stomach. Tarimev, again, deflected the attack on him but this time thrust forward with his sword and drove it through the man's chest. The pirate dropped his sword and clutched his wound before falling to his knees. Tarimev seized the opportunity, slashed his sword horizontally and opened the pirate's throat, finishing him off. The pirate captain screamed in anger. He attacked Tarimev with a flurry of blows from his sword, all of which Tarimev managed to deflect. The captain swung his unarmed hand and connected his fist with Tarimev's jaw. Tarimev stumbled backwards, blood trickling from his mouth. The captain charged at him with his sword held high above his head. Tarimev blocked the attack with his sword and swung his left arm around in an attempt to strike the captain in the side of the head. He moved aside just in time and Tarimev's strike flew wide.

The captain punched Tarimev in the side of the head, sending him stumbling backward before tripping to the ground. He kicked Tarimev in the ribs and stomped on his stomach, then placed his boot on Tarimev's chest and pressed down, pinning him to the floor and crushing his ribcage. Tarimev could see a battle forming all around them as the city guards fought back against the pirate crew who had been hidden amongst the crowd.

"You're going to regret ever crossing me," the captain snarled. He raised his foot to stamp down on Tarimev again. Tarimev prepared for the pain and the incoming impact, when a figure tackled the pirate from the side. Tarimev sat up and looked over to see Torvald wrestling with captain. They were both on the ground wrestling each other until Torvald forced the captain onto his back. The pirate kicked Torvald off him with both his legs and quickly stood. He picked up his cutlass and pointed it at both of the recruits.

"Don't think I won't kill you," he growled, "You shouldn't be getting in my way."

The pirate captain glanced over to look at his sailor, dead on the ground, before he looked back at the two friends. "Where is the Princess?" he demanded.

"Staying away from you," Torvald snarled back, as he stood next to Tarimev and drew his sword. The three men had just begun to duel when another pirate ran over and put herself between the three combatants, pushing her captain away from the fight.

She was a girl of Tarimev's age, her bright red hair looking like flames in the sun. She was remarkably pale and clean for someone who lived on a ship as a pirate. She had a pistol in one hand and a sword in the other. Her slender frame and pointed ears showed that, as an elf, her age was deceiving and she was likely much older.

"Captain, they're overwhelming us," she cried, "We need to leave."

The captain looked at the girl, then at Tarimev and Torvald, before turning back to the girl.

"If we leave, we'll have failed. Rally the crew and finish them off. The King wants the Princess."

He pushed his way past the girl and continued advancing, but as he neared the two recruits, Tarimev took a step forward and lunged forward with his sword. He took the captain unawares and the tip of his blade caught the left side of the captain's abdomen. Tarimev stepped closer to his foe and drove the blade deeper. As Tarimev withdrew the blade, the pirate stepped back in shock and placed his hand over the wound. Another two pirates ran in, barging the two recruits aside and grabbing their captain under his arms.

"Aylu, we have to leave now!" one of them shouted as they dragged him away.

"No! You can't do this!" shouted the captain, who Tarimev realised must be Aylu.

"Captain, he's right," the girl said, "This is our only chance of escape."

Aylu struggled in their grasp but it was no use, he was overpowered. The girl pulled her pistol from its holster and fired it into the air as a signal.

Within minutes, the pirates were back on their ship and the sails were set to take them away from the port.

Tarimev and Torvald watched them leave port, then sheathed their swords and made their way back to the princess.

After a short walk, they arrived back at the town hall. A crowd had gathered outside, trying to escape the battle. They saw Tarimev and Torvald return to the building and cheered for them. The two of them entered the building to find Princess Cayte waiting with the captain of the city guard, Darin, in the entrance room.

"I'm so glad you're safe," said the Princess and she embraced Torvald in a hug before quickly letting him go.

"Thank you, Your Highness," replied Torvald, shifting his stance slightly awkwardly.

"What happened out there?" asked the captain of the guard.

"Your men fought well, and with their help we drove the pirates away," replied Tarimev.

"That was brave of you," said the Princess, "I am sorry that you had to fight like that."

"It's our job, Your Majesty," Torvald said with a smile and a bow, "We would give our lives to keep you safe." As Torvald rose from his bow, Tarimev could almost swear his friend winked at the Princess.

"Well, I appreciate it nonetheless," said the Princess, "Did either of you see Sergeant Galeren? He hasn't returned yet."

"No. We haven't seen him since before the attack," replied Tarimev.

"I hope nothing has happened to him," the Princess said, "He's been through so much already."

"I'm sure nothing has happened to him, Your Majesty," Torvald said, trying to reassure her, "he's a fine soldier. He will be okay."

"I had better return to my room," Princess Cayte said, the worry still strong in her voice, "You two should go and rest."

"Of course, Your Highness, we will return you to Alerill in the morning," Torvald said, bowing again.

"Thank you. Both of you," she said, "You've done very well today."

She walked away and the two recruits left the town hall and headed back to the site of the battle.

Once they arrived back at the port square, Torvald left Tarimev to help with the clean-up whilst he spoke to one of the guards. After a few moments, he returned to Tarimev.

"We did less than we thought it seems, the only pirate we managed to kill is the one that you killed. They killed many more of the city guard than expected as well. I think they only fled because they thought we might kill their Captain."

"They'll be back," said Tarimev.

"I'm sure they will. I would have thought it won't be for a while though. I'm afraid there is more bad news."

"More bad news?"

"Yes, Sergeant Galeren didn't make it. The city guard found his body amongst the dead. From his wounds, it seems he put up a good fight."

"Oh gods," said Tarimev, "I'm sorry to hear that.

May Eterna guide him to safety."

"Amen to that."

"I suppose we should return and prepare to take the Princess home."

"We can prepare in the morning. I, for one, am going to recover for the rest of the day. Finish helping out here and I will see you in the morning."

Torvald turned and left Tarimev on his own. Tarimev helped with the rest of the clean-up before he left the square and made his way to the inn he spent the previous evening in. He enjoyed two ales and a meal of unknown meat with cabbage before he left. He strolled through the streets of the town for the rest of the afternoon before he made his way back to the town hall.

It was late evening when Tarimev returned to the town hall and walked through the main room into the area reserved for guests. As he walked to his room he passed the dining hall, where he saw a feast taking place. Captain Darin saw him and called him over.

"Come and join us, you must be tired after all the excitement," said Captain Darin.

"I don't think so, Captain," replied Tarimev, "I'm going to bed."

"Go to bed after. Have some food and some fun. You won't regret it."

Tarimev followed Darin into the dining hall and sat down at the table. He was served a plate of roast chicken and vegetables, which he ate slowly, enjoying every mouthful. He washed it down with ale and wine until he felt pleasantly full.

The captain stood up and hit his tankard with his

fork to announce a speech.

"Ladies and gentlemen," he began, "we are here tonight to celebrate the victory against the pirates, and although we mourn the loss of our friends, we also thank the knights who came to our aid this day. Without them, we would not have turned our foes away. I know that Mr Storheam was not able to be here but, in his stead, we thank you, Mr Riswaell."

Tarimev looked around the hall and smiled, nodding at the soldiers.

"And now, let us drink to the memory of our fallen comrades!" Darin shouted, "To the fallen heroes of Herfeld!"

All the soldiers cheered and raised their tankards. Tarimev joined in the toast and drank deeply. He sat back in his chair and watched the festivities continue for a little longer before he left the hall.

He made his way back to his room and lay down on the bed. It took mere minutes for him to drift off into much needed sleep.

11

The city guard loaded all the princess's items onto her carriage whilst she ate breakfast with Tarimev and Torvald. Captain Darin sat with them and assured the princess that Sergeant Galeren's body would be sent to Alerill in the coming days.

"Thank you, Captain," she said, "I shall mourn his loss greatly, he was a good friend to me."

"It is a difficult job we do, Your Highness. We can only hope that one day the sort of scum that carry out these attacks go the way of the Orcs. Until then, we will continue to serve our king and country to the best of our ability."

"And I thank you for your service, Captain," said the Princess, "and please thank the mayor for his hospitality these past days."

Captain Darin bowed and left them, and soon after the Princess and her protectors were on their way back to Alerill. The rest of the day passed by uneventfully, but by the time they made camp, Cayte found herself unable to sleep over fears that the men who came for her might still be nearby. Torvald and Tarimev were equally restless and so the three of them spent the night staying awake, talking around the campfire. They discussed what they had seen at the market and how the attack on the princess had been carried out.

"What if they are planning another attempt?" Tarimev spoke, "We have no idea where they went or when they'll strike again."

"That's true, but we know enough that we can tell the King and he will provide more men for her protection," Torvald said facing the princess.

"My father has already done more than enough," said Cayte, "but I appreciate your concern nonetheless."

"I'm just worried about you," said Torvald. "I wouldn't know what to do if any harm came to you, Cayte."

Princess Cayte blushed, swept her loose hair behind her ear and sheepishly looked away from him.

"Thank you, Torvald. I should hope we never come to that eventuality," she let out a yawn, "I think I am going to retire now, maybe knowing the both of you are watching over me will help me sleep."

"Goodnight, Princess," said Tarimev.

Cayte nodded and crawled into her bedroll. She lay there for some time before finally drifting off.

She dreamed of the port attack, of the pirates that had attacked her, and of the man who stood at her side, protecting her from the vicious onslaught. In her dream, she could see the gleam of the sun reflecting off the blade of his sword, and she knew it was her knight.

Meanwhile, once the Princess had disappeared into her tent, Tarimev turned to his friend and said, "What the hell was that, Torvald? That wasn't very professional."

Torvald shrugged and replied, "What do you mean?"

"You know damn well what I mean, calling the princess by her name instead of her title! If Sergeant Koln had heard that he would have kicked you out of your training!"

"It was a slip of the tongue, nothing more. Don't get so stressed about it."

Tarimev sighed and said, "Look, we've grown close over these past two years, you're my best friend and I love you like a brother, but you need to be careful with her. She's royalty, not someone to be spoken to as an equal. It's disrespectful and you can't afford to disrespect anyone right now."

"I know, I know, but I didn't mean anything by it. It's just -"

"Just what?" Tarimev interrupted. "Just that you like her? You want to take her as your wife? Is that what this is all about?"

"Maybe I do!" Torvald shouted as he stood up from his seat. "I have grown close to her over my training and in all honesty, I love her, and I just hope that she feels the same way. But you have to admit that she is beautiful, strong and intelligent. Why shouldn't I want to marry her?"

"Because you're a common soldier and she's a princess," said Tarimev, "You're not even a full-fledged soldier yet, you're a trainee. She is supposed to marry a nobleman, someone of high standing, not a lowly soldier."

"Why should she be forced to marry someone that she doesn't want to just because of standing? Anyway, that doesn't matter, thanks to my parents I'm actually considered a noble."

"I thought your parents were merchants?"

"They started off as merchants but as their company grew, they eventually became nobility. My father owns the land that Calramon sits and runs the city alongside my mother."

Tarimev hummed. "That's impressive."

"Yes, it is, but I'm not going to use that as an excuse to try and force her into marriage, and I don't want you telling people about it. I want to advance my career without relying on my family's achievements. I have no interest in being associated with them."

"I get your point, my friend. Just make sure that your affections aren't one-sided before they potentially ruin your career. You wouldn't want to become a laughing stock, now would you?"

"No, I suppose not."

"Now go to sleep, I'll keep watch for the rest of the night so you can be well-rested for your day of flirting tomorrow," Tarimev smirked as he finished speaking.

Torvald rolled his eyes and gave a quick nod before walking back towards the tent. He was thankful that his friend had been understanding.

Tarimev now sat alone at the campfire. He couldn't believe what his friend had confessed to him. He suspected that Torvald liked the princess, but he hadn't expected him to say anything about it. Now he felt responsible for the consequences that may arise from such a confession. He decided he wouldn't begrudge his friend's feelings though, for he now knew how his friend felt. He thought back to his time in Burtop; ever since he had first developed an attraction to the opposite sex it had seemed like there was a new love for him every week. A pretty girl only had to speak to him nicely and he would find himself in love with her. But as he grew older, he learned the difference between love and infatuation, and nowadays he would take quite a bit of persuading to proceed with any romantic endeavours. As far as he was concerned, the gods had a plan for him and he would find what they intended for him eventually, but searching for it was a mistake. He laughed at himself, knowing that if he continued to ponder on the subject, he would just worry, instead, he poured himself some wine and began sharpening his sword. Within a few hours, his sword was sharp, his armour was polished, and his pistol was clean. He tried to think of another way to pass the time when he heard hoofbeats approaching from the distance.

The next morning, Torvald woke from a deeper sleep than he had managed the past night. The first thing he thought about was whether Cayte had heard everything he said last night. She was certainly pretty and he was sure that the secret trysts they had had been having over the past six months showed that she had feelings for him. However, he doubted that she would want to marry him. She was a noblewoman, and as far as she knew, he was a common soldier, she would probably prefer someone with higher status than that.

He sat up from his bedroll and stretched his arms above his head. His muscles ached slightly after sleeping on the hard ground, but he felt refreshed nonetheless. He stepped out of his tent, dressed in just his trousers, only to see a full troop of soldiers standing around the campfire. They were all in their full armour, each holding a shield, spear or sword.

"What's going on?" asked Torvald.

"Mr Storheam, good morning. King Occime received word of the attack in Herfeld. We were sent to aid your escort of the princess," replied one of the soldiers.

"Where is Tarimev?"

"He has gone with our Sergeant to scout the road ahead. They should be returning soon."

Torvald recognised some of the soldiers that were milling about so he nodded and went back inside his tent to get dressed. He took a moment to check his equipment, making sure that his armour was undamaged. He pulled on his boots and tightened the buckle. When he emerged from the tent again, he saw that Tarimev and the Sergeant had returned. The Sergeant approached Torvald and reached out to shake his hand.

"Good to meet you, Storheam. I am Sergeant Kaeshi, I trust you slept well?"

"As well as I could in a tent."

Kaeshi laughed and said, "We've got a long way to travel today, so we need to move quickly. The road ahead seemed clear but we can never be too careful. I defer my command to you for the rest of this mission, I was informed before we came that this is your trial."

"Thank you, Sergeant. I will wake the princess, and then we should move ahead. I plan on continuing back to Alerill via a longer route, so we should arrive back by nightfall."

"Very well, lead on. If you have any problems just let me know."

Torvald entered the Princess's tent and roused her gently. She sat up slowly and rubbed her eyes, looking around the tent in confusion.

"My lady, are you ready to depart?"

"Yes, yes, of course." She replied hastily, "give me a moment to get dressed."

Torvald nodded and turned to leave the tent, but he was surprised when he felt a hand grab his shoulder. He looked back to see the princess smiling at him, her cheeks flushed and her brown eyes sparkling.

"By the way, Torvald, I love you too." She smirked and lightly kissed him on his cheek, "now go, let me get dressed."

Torvald blushed and left the tent. He was embarrassed at being caught off guard like that, but he was also relieved that there was clearly a future with Cayte for him. He left the tent and began issuing commands to the nearby soldiers, having them take down the tents and load up the carriage. It took only half an hour to get everything packed away and ready to depart.

The Princess boarded her carriage, and Tarimev sat in the driver's seat. Torvald went to mount a spare horse to lead the group when he heard the Princess call out to him.

"Wait!"

He stopped and waited for her to approach him.

"I would feel much safer with you in the carriage with me, Mr Storheam."

Torvald nodded and dismounted from his horse. He briefly told his planned route to Sergeant Kaeshi, and then walked past Tarimev on his way to the carriage door. He could barely hold his laugh when Tarimev smirked and winked at him.

Torvald opened the carriage door and climbed inside. The Princess smiled at him and motioned for him to sit beside her.

Sergeant Kaeshi set off, leading the group towards Alerill.

The sun rose high in the sky and cast its light upon the world. The land was mostly flat and unbroken except for the occasional hill or large tree. Occasionally there would be a farmhouse or collection of buildings, but other than that the journey was uneventful. As dusk began to draw in, Tarimev spotted the unmistakable city walls of Alerill. He guided the carriage to the gate and they were waved through the gate by the soldiers on the wall.

The Festival of Menobe was in full swing in the capital still, and the streets were crowded with people and carts, with the smell of food permeating the air. They passed several taverns and inns, each livelier than the last. They continued past the festivities and into the palace grounds where there were more guards than usual. The Princess' carriage was greeted by the King's private guard, known as the King's Protectorate.

The Princess was escorted to her room, which was a large suite of rooms overlooking the palace gardens. Tarimev and Torvald were asked to wait in the Grand

Hall while the Princess changed into a fresh dress and then joined them. They waited for a few moments before the grand doors opened at the end of the hall and the King and Queen entered the room, with Sergeant Koln behind them.

Queen Lorea was an older woman, perhaps in her late fifties. She was still very attractive, with dark hair and a strong face. She was dressed in a simple purple gown, with a red scarf tied around her neck.

The King looked at the two men and gave a small nod. "Welcome home, Princess Cayte."

Cayte curtsied and smiled at the King.

Queen Lorea approached her and took her hand in hers as she smiled warmly at her daughter before embracing her.

"It is good to see you again my dear, you look well. Considering -"

She was interrupted by her husband who spoke next.

"We are glad you're safe, Cayte."

Cayte bowed her head slightly.

"Thank you, Father."

The King then turned to Torvald and gave him a slight bow.

"And you too, Sir Storheam."

Torvald returned the King's bow and said "Your Majesty, it is a pleasure to see you again. However, with the greatest respect, I must correct you - I am not yet a Knight, only a trainee. I should be addressed as mister."

The King chuckled. "I appreciate the correction, but I *was* correct. Kneel."

Torvald did so and the King drew his sword and

held it over Torvald's head, "Torvald Storheam, do you swear to serve the Kingdom of Alerill and protect all within it?"

Torvald felt his heart racing and he knew what was coming. "I swear."

The King tapped the flat of his blade on Torvald's shoulder before he put it back in its scabbard and gave him a small smile.

"You may rise, Sir Torvald Storheam, Knight of the King's Army of Worthervir."

Torvald stood up and the King smiled at him. "Congratulations, Sir Storheam. Sergeant Koln, I believe you had something to say."

Koln cleared his throat. "Thank you, Your Highness. Sir Storheam, I was charged with training you and your companions. I have taught you the basics of soldiering and you have shown great skill. Your prowess has been proven time and time again over the past two years and your defence of the princess has further shown this." Koln drew his sword and held it out in front of him, the blade resting on the palm of his hand. "As the first man to be knighted from this troop, it is my honour to bestow upon you this sword. I hope it serves you throughout your career as well as it served me." Torvald graciously accepted the weapon, a rush of pride instantly filled him.

"Thank you, Sergeant."

"You deserve it. Now go, enjoy the evening. Tomorrow afternoon report to the palace for your posting."

Torvald saluted the Sergeant, then bowed to the King and Queen and said, "Thank you, Your Majesty."

He turned to Cayte and said, "It was a pleasure

serving you, Your Highness."

Cayte curtsied, "I am sure we shall meet again soon."

Tarimev followed Torvald's lead, saluted the Sergeant, bowed to the Royal Family and turned to leave. "Mr Riswaell, come to my office tomorrow afternoon," Koln shouted after him.

He stopped and looked back at Koln, "Yes, Sergeant."

The two friends left the Grand Hall and made their way out of the palace.

"Well done, Sir Torvald," Tarimev said with pride as they walked the corridors.

"Thanks, Tarimev. I'm sure it will be your turn soon."

"Well, the Sergeant wants to see me tomorrow so you never know," Tarimev laughed at himself, "Enough of work, let's get to the festival, we should celebrate for you."

They reached the main entrance and stepped outside into the evening air.

12

Torvald and Tarimev left the palace and headed towards the city centre. As they passed through the palace grounds, they saw a large crowd gathered near the gates. They got closer to the people and the sound of loud music and people laughing could be heard.

"Sounds like the festival is in full swing," Tarimev said with excitement.

"I think you're right, it's almost time for the fireworks."

Before they left the grounds, they found a spot near the stage where they could watch the show, seated near the highest dignitaries of the realm. Tarimev was amazed at how many people were present to celebrate the festival. He wondered what other festivals there were in this world and if one day he might see them all.

While lost in thought, a servant brought him and

Torvald a goblet of wine each, which broke Tarimev out of his daydreaming. "Thank you," he said with appreciation as he took the drink from the servant.

Darkness finally fell and the King's sorcerer stepped onto the stage, accompanied by trumpets and drums. With a deep breath, he began casting a spell and lit up the sky with an explosion of colour that filled everyone's hearts with joy. For an hour, the crowd stared, enraptured, as he cast incantation after incantation, filling the air with magic. Green beams cast into the sky before exploding into giant stars, red sparks erupting hundreds of feet into the air. Every time he cast a spell the lights would fade only to be replaced by another barrage of colours and sounds. It was a beautiful display. Being from a small village, Tarimev had never seen proper sorcery before, and so he watched with childlike awe. Eventually, the sorcerer finished his display and stepped off stage while the crowd erupted into applause. Tarimev and Torvald joined in with the crowd's applause until the sorcerer waved his hand and the sconces on the stage immediately extinguished themselves. The crowd grew quiet as the sound of the drums faded away.

"I've always loved the closing ceremonies of these festivals. Come on, let's enjoy the last night of festivities," Torvald said, grabbing Tarimev's arm and pulling him along.

They left the palace grounds and wandered into the city. The streets were lined with stalls outside every shop, and where there was no shop, there was a stall anyway. Tables filled the street selling food and drinks. Tarimev couldn't believe his eyes; the whole place was so lively. Games were being played everywhere. People sat around tables playing cards, others were playing dice and a few were even gambling.

The two friends walked down the main road and stopped in front of a large tent. It was decorated with colourful banners and flags. Inside, people were dancing and drinking.

"What do you think?" Torvald asked, "You want to go in?"

"Absolutely!" Tarimev replied excitedly.

They stepped inside the tent and it was packed with people. They made their way to the back and found a table big enough for both of them. Torvald ordered some drinks and then turned to Tarimev.

"So, how are you liking your first festival?" he asked.

"It's amazing! I don't know what I expected, but it wasn't this. All these people here enjoying themselves; it's incredible."

"You've really never been to one before?" he asked.

Tarimev shook his head, "No, never. Whenever there was something like this, I had to help my dad with the farm. I never got the chance to enjoy a party like this."

He looked at Torvald, "And you? I take it you had these festivals back in Calramon?"

"All the time. I never got to enjoy them like this though, I always had to make a good impression for my parents."

"Well not tonight, my friend. Tonight, you can drink and dance to your heart's content." Tarimev raised his tankard to Torvald.

Torvald smiled at Tarimev, "I'll drink to that." They clinked their tankards together and drank to the occasion. They were soon joining in with the rest of the festival-goers, dancing to the music in the middle of the tent. Tarimev danced with different girls, none of whom he managed to catch the name of.

As the night wore on, Torvald grew tired. "I'll have to call it a night here I'm afraid, I have to be ready for my first duty by tomorrow afternoon."

Tarimev looked disappointed, "Well take care, my friend. I'm sure we will see each other again soon."

Tarimev continued to drink and dance after Torvald left. He carried on until the early hours of the morning, when the festival came to an end and the ale ran out. As he staggered out of the tent, one of the girls he had danced with earlier in the night grabbed him by the arm and said "Come on, the taverns are still open. The night isn't over yet." He remembered her voice from earlier but in his state, he could barely make out her face.

She pulled him towards a tavern she knew of and led him through the streets until they arrived. She told him to sit wherever he liked as she went off to get drinks. She returned with two tankards of ale and sat next to Tarimev.

"My name is Nelka," she said, "but my friends call me Nelly."

Tarimev smiled and nodded, "Nice to meet you, Nelly. My name's Tarimev."

Nelly laughed, "I like the way you say it!"

The two talked for a while, and the more they drank the more they shared about each other.

The Trials of Knights

Eventually, Nelka was telling him about her childhood, but Tarimev realised he could hear the conversation of the men at the table behind Nelly.

"Ya shoulda been there, it was chaos. They didn't expect us at all. If the Knights weren't passing through, we woulda destroyed the whole village," one of the men said, "I nearly got caught meself, Shrave here got me away in time." He pointed to a man sitting on the other side of the table.

"I bet you're glad he did," another man replied. "If he hadn't arrived in time, you would be in jail as well."

Tarimev was snapped back into his conversation when Nelly snapped her fingers in front of his face and said, "Hey, where'd you go? Were you even listening to me?"

"Sorry, I got distracted by the people behind you." She looked over her shoulder to take a look at them, "Oh, you mean Shrave? He's a proper villain. He was part of an attack on some village nearby some time ago." The man she called Shrave was a tall man, at least a foot taller than Tarimev even sitting down. He wore an open vest which showed a body of pure muscle covered in scars, and his shaved head and face proudly displayed his facial scars.

"You don't mean Burtop, do you?" Tarimev asked.

"Yes, that's right. He likes to get drunk and brag about it. I suppose it's been a few years now."

"Two years."

"You know abou-" Tarimev stood from the table before Nelly finished her question and sat with the men behind him.

"So, you're the infamous bandits who attacked Burtop?" Tarimev asked.

"Well, I suppose we *are* infamous now, aren't we?"

Shrave laughed to his friend before looking Tarimev in the eyes, "Don't worry, we won't tell anyone if you don't."

Tarimev joined him with a false laugh, "No need to worry about that. How involved with the attack were you?"

"I was supposed to cause as much damage as possible. Did quite well, managed to kill a couple of them, and then I burned down all their crops and their farmhouse."

"That was you?" Tarimev snarled through gritted teeth.

"Yep, I was the one lit the fire," Shrave said proudly, unaware of the change in Tarimev's demeanour. The sound of the rest of the tavern seemed to drown away as Tarimev stared at the man who destroyed his childhood home. All other thoughts left his head as he threw himself over the table and tackled Shrave off of his chair.

They rolled across the floor; fists flying and feet kicking as Shrave tried to gain the upper hand. He was larger than Tarimev and easily strong enough to overpower him. The two got back onto their feet and Shrave's next punch landed on Tarimev's cheekbone, sending him flying through the air and onto a table, where he blacked out for a moment.

When he awoke, he saw Shrave standing above him. He scrambled to his feet and attempted to strike the man, but his arms felt numb and his legs too weak to support him. Shrave simply caught his fist and started to twist Tarimev's arm away from his body. He leaned in close to Tarimev and whispered "You made a big fuckin' mistake kid, and now you're gonna pay." He twisted harder until Tarimev cried out in pain and collapsed to his knees. Tarimev looked around for anything that could help him when he saw a smashed bottle of what was once rum next to him from when he landed on the table. Before he had the chance to grab it, the door of the tavern burst open and two knights stood there with their swords out. "Drop the boy, and surrender!" A knight yelled.

Shrave complied and dropped Tarimev to the floor. Tarimev picked up the bottle and clambered to his feet. He was now standing face-to-face with the man who destroyed his family home, and apart from his sword, robbed him of all ties he had to his father. In a mixture of drunkenness and rage, Tarimev slammed the jagged end of the bottle into Shrave's chest. Blood poured from the wound and splashed Tarimev's face. Shrave let out a cry of agony and blood seeped out of his wound, coating both the bottle and Tarimev's hand.

Shrave fell backwards onto the floor, clutching his chest and screaming. Tarimev reached out to remove the bottle from Shrave's chest, and then attacked again, further goring his enemy's chest.

The knights ran forward and grabbed Tarimev whose only focus was on his enemy. They pinned his arms behind him and clamped shackles around his wrists. Shrave gurgled as his last breath left him, his eyes wide with fear as the life fled from his body and he lay still. The adrenaline left Tarimev, and he suddenly felt all the drink he had had over the night.

"What the hell happened here?" One of the knights asked.

Tarimev laughed, "A stupid... A stupid idiot ruined my home, I thought I'd kill... hurt him."

"How much ale have you had?"

"Wait a second, I know you. You were with us when we arrested Captain Nirel." The other knight said, he then looked at his ally. "Huchon, you recognise him?"

"Yeah, I think I do actually. You're a recruit?" Huchon asked.

"Yes, I am," Tarimev stood proudly, "Recruit Riswaell at your service."

"Can I ask why you killed him?"

"He burnt down my farm. Destroyed all of my possessions."

"Right, well we have to take you to the jail, recruit. We will inform your commanding officer who will then inform the King and the Marçhal ambassador. They will confer and determine your punishment."

The knights led Tarimev out of the tavern and led him through the streets as he staggered along with them, keeping his head down in hopes of not being recognised.

He had no idea how long they walked before they stopped outside a building. Tarimev was placed inside a cell, which was just large enough for him and a small undressed bed. It was cold and damp, and he felt like he was going to be sick.

"We need your armour and your sword please." Huchon said to him.

"Is it really necessary? I don't think I'll be using them anytime soon." Tarimev said, trying to lighten the mood.

The guard laughed and slapped him on the shoulder. "It's to make sure you don't escape. Don't worry, you won't have much time to get used to being locked up."

Tarimev removed his armour and weapons belt and handed them over. He wasn't in the mood to argue or fight, as he figured it would be futile.

The knights shut the iron grate door and locked Tarimev in the cell. He sat on his bed and rested his head against the wall, regretting all of the decisions he had made tonight.

His mind drifted to his father. He remembered the day he died, and the day after, when he woke up and realised he wouldn't see his father again. He remembered working the fields with his father, and he missed those long days under the sun for the first time in his life. With more thought, he considered how his father would have felt if he saw him now. He had brought shame to the family name. Cosai wanted a simple life for his son, and now Tarimev sat in a cell for getting the revenge he had dreamt of, but he didn't feel different. In fact, it only felt worse than before. And as he pondered, the drink finally began to take hold of him, and he passed out.

13

For the first time in the past two years, Tarimev awoke without his partner in the bunk next to his. He looked out the window and saw the sun had only just risen past the point of dawn horizon. Another wave of remorse washed over him when he thought about how he had taken a life the night before. He had killed before in the line of duty, but always in defence of himself or others. Last night he made the first move, something he never imagined he'd do. He heard his name shouted from down the corridor as someone unlocked his cell door. A guard stood there with Sergeant Koln beside him.

"Your weapons and armour are in the guard's room. Go get dressed and then come back to the barracks," growled Sergeant Koln whilst Tarimev looked up at him, "We need to talk."

Tarimev got out of bed and went to get his clothes

on. He finished getting dressed, put his armour on, left the town jail blocks and walked back towards the barracks.

When he got there, he found the Sergeant sitting behind his desk looking over some papers. He waved his hand, indicating that Tarimev should shut the door. Clearly he wanted to talk privately, which meant that whatever they were talking about was probably bad news.

"Come in," Koln said. His voice was as calm as it ever was, but the look on his face told Tarimev everything he needed to know.

"Sir?" Tarimev asked.

The sergeant looked up from his paperwork and leaned forward. "I was not happy to be woken in the dead of night to the news of your escapades last night. I understand what happened in broad terms, but I want to hear exactly how it all went down."

Tarimev took a deep breath. He wished he could lie and tell the Sergeant that the man made the first move and that it was all self-defence, but the truth would have to come out eventually. He explained everything, the entire events of the night, down to the most minute detail. After he was done, Koln sat back in his chair, drumming his fingers on the desktop.

"So now I'm left wondering, why didn't you arrest him? If I remember correctly, you're almost a trained soldier, are you not? For Vaysan's sake, Tarimev, I was going to give you your trial today."

Tarimev sighed. "I know what I did was wrong, Sir. I regretted my actions immediately, but my emotions got the better of me. He destroyed the only connection that I had left with my father."

The Sergeant shook his head. "That doesn't excuse your actions, Tarimev. Killing is never an option unless it's absolutely necessary, and even then, it must be done with the utmost precision. However, you are lucky. Somehow, Princess Cayte has also heard of the events of last night and has come to your defence. With that in mind, and after an audience with King Occime and Marçhal Bergan this morning, we have decided how we will proceed with this matter."

"What is that, Sergeant?"

"You have a quest. I don't know the details, but we will be going to see Marçhal Bergan shortly who will brief you on the details. The key points to remember are these; if you succeed in this quest, you'll be made a King's Knight and granted a full pardon. If you fail, or refuse to take it, you will be expelled from the training program and will face a criminal trial on the death of the man last night."

Tarimev's eyes widened at the mention of a trial. He couldn't imagine himself facing a court martial if he refused to accept, but that was what he had to consider.

"Are you ready to go, then?" Koln asked.

"Yes, Sergeant," Tarimev replied dryly.

Koln stood up and motioned towards the door with his hand, Tarimev led the way out of the office and out into the streets. They walked in silence, heading towards the Palace where they would meet with Marçhal Bergan and the King. As they made their way into the palace grounds, Koln turned to Tarimev and said, "If you can forget that I am your sergeant for a moment, I hope this goes well for you, son. I shouldn't say this, but you and Torvald have been my favourite recruits I've ever had the fortune of training over the years. You are one of the best men I know."

Tarimev smiled. "Thank you, Sergeant. Thank you very much."

They walked the rest of the way in silence until they reached the meeting hall. The room was a large round room with a round oak table in the centre, adorned with the crest of Worthervir. The walls had banners in the colours of the nation, and sitting on an ornate throne at the table was King Occime. In the chair to his left was Marçhal Bergan, and Sergeant Koln left Tarimev's side to take a seat on the King's right. The King motioned to the seat opposite him and said, "Please sit, Mr Riswaell."

Tarimev bowed to the King and then did as he was told. He wasn't sure what to expect next so he waited patiently, trying to look as official as possible. Eventually, the King spoke, "When I first met you, I thought greatly of you. You seemed like you would be an excellent addition to my soldiers. But the news I have heard of last night has not only damaged that opinion, but it will also damage the people's opinion of the Knights of Worthervir. I will be honest with you, once I heard about a knight being arrested off-duty I was ready to send you straight to a criminal trial, not least because it meant I had to attend a meeting with my council in the early hours of the morning. However, my daughter heard what was going on and defended you. You should be thanking her that you are getting the opportunity you are getting right now. I trust that Sergeant Koln has already informed you of what we are going to do with you, yes?"

Tarimev nodded.

"Good. Well then let us begin." The King leaned forwards in his chair and rested his elbows on the table. "This quest we are sending you on is a very dangerous one, and the likelihood that you will die is very high, but if you succeed then I will make sure that your little indiscretion last night is legitimised. Marçhal Bergan, would you tell Mr Riswaell what he will be attempting?"

Bergan stood up and placed a map on the table in front of Tarimev. "This quest will take you into the Yevanti Wilds. I have performed some rituals and detected signs of dark magic in the Ashen Mountain, deep in the heart of the Wilds. We think that a necromancer has taken up residence there. Your job will be to investigate this, and if there is a dark magician, kill them. You will need permission from the Yevanti to travel through their lands. Go to their city of Qoan and request passage, but be careful, they are dangerous barbarians. Be wary of their warriors, they are trained to fight."

Tarimev raised his eyebrows, "A necromancer? I thought that sort of magic died out when the orcs did."

The Marçhal shook his head "No, the necromancy still exists, it is simply less refined than what the orc tribes used to practice. When the orcs went extinct, the majority of necromantic knowledge was lost with them. This magic that we have detected is the strongest dark magic we have seen in a long time."

"With respect, is this not a task better suited to a Marçhal?"

"It would have been, but we are not even certain that the necromancer exists, and his majesty needed a punishment for you."

"Well then, I shall leave for Qoan as soon as I can," Tarimev said, "Is there anything else I should know before I leave?"

The King waved his hand dismissively. "You know everything we know. Your horse is prepared at the palace stables. Be careful Mr Riswaell, and for your sake, I hope you are successful."

"I will be, Sire," Tarimev replied.

He rose to his feet, thanking the King and Marçhal Bergan for allowing him to prove himself before leaving the room. As soon as he was out of sight, he let out a sigh of relief, until the reality of what he was being asked to face dawned on him.

He rode for a few hours along the main road out of Alerill. He passed several small holdings, but none of them were large enough to draw any attention. His mind was filled with thoughts of the dangers ahead, and thinking back to his training, he remembered how to deal with various types of weapons and how to fight effectively. He knew that he could handle himself in combat, even against a necromancer.

Finally, after riding along the main road for some time, he turned onto a smaller track. It was narrow and windy, passing between low hills covered in dense forest. He decided to stop for a moment for some food as, he realised, he hadn't eaten since the night before. He took bread, cheese and dried meat from his pack and began to eat. He gave his horse some grain and water as well. After eating, he mounted his horse and set off again, continuing toward the Yevanti Wilds. As he rode, lost in his own head, he heard a shout for help from further down the road. He kicked his mount into a gallop and continued towards the sound until he saw a young man lying on the ground. It looked like he had been assaulted, and he was bleeding heavily from a wound to his chest. Tarimev spurred his horse forward and dismounted quickly, then ran to the injured man's side and knelt beside him. "Are you alright?" he asked, looking down at the wounded man.

"Oh, thank you!" the man gasped, grasping Tarimev's hand and squeezing it tightly. "I don't know how much longer I can hold on," he said, blood bubbling between his lips.

Tarimev grimaced as he realised that the man probably had only minutes left to live, yet he was still alive. "Tell me about yourself," he said, hoping to give the man some company in his final moments.

"My name is Sivik," he groaned in pain as he clutched his chest, "Sivik Mosta, I'm a fortune-teller from Ropeh. My wife and three children are back home waiting for me." Tears started forming in his eyes as he continued talking.

"Nice to meet you Sivik. Tell me about your family."

"They're my everything. I love them more than anything in the world," he said, tears streaming down his face. "I was going to take them to Askerskali next month. The kids have always wanted to see the garden city."

"You'll take them there," Tarimev promised him, trying to ignore the large gash across his chest that was pouring blood. He put his fingers inside the wound and tried to stop the bleeding.

"Thank you!" Sivik gasped again, the tears flowing

freely now. "Please, please tell them I love them, and I'm sorry I couldn't see them grow."

Tarimev wiped the tears away from Sivik's eyes and said "There's no need for that, Sivik. You've done nothing wrong; you mustn't feel guilty."

"I should have been a better husband," Sivik sobbed, "I should have made her happy."

"You were a good husband," Tarimev assured him, "and a great father. I'm sure she knows that. Just tell them that you love them and that they will always be proud of you."

"Please be truthful, I won't make it will I? Just tell me the truth…" the words trailed off as he groaned, then coughed violently and blood sprayed from his mouth. His breathing grew more laboured and he began to fade away. Tarimev felt his soul begin to crumble as he watched the man's body fall limp in his arms when the life drained out of him. Tarimev bowed his head and let out silent tears; even though he didn't know Sivik in life, to view a man so desperate to avoid death was a painful thing. He brushed his fingers over Sivik's eyes to close them and sat in silence for a moment. Suddenly, Sivik opened his eyes again, and although they were pure black, he looked at Tarimev as though he could see him clearly.

"They are not gone," Sivik whispered with a breathless voice, "They will return, and there will be war. You must be prepared." His eyes returned to the green they were before and his body went limp again.

Tarimev stood up and looked around, wondering if anyone had heard Sivik's last words. A short distance away he saw a small dried-up pond with a thicket of trees behind it; this would do nicely for a burial. He carried the body over and covered it with handfuls of grass and leaves. Once he was finished, he placed a stone on top of the grave. He then headed back to the road and continued on his way. He thought about Sivik's words and wondered what he meant. Who was returning? He thought it best not to dwell on it, as there would be plenty of time to think later, once he had completed his quest.

A few more hours passed and Tarimev began to see the trees of the Yevanti Wilds in the distance. Rather than risk another attack like the last time he was here, he decided to camp before he reached the forest. He led his horse off the track and into a field where there was plenty of space to set up a tent. With the sun setting and the temperature dropping rapidly, he quickly built a fire and sat around it to keep warm. As he waited for his stew to cook, his mind piled with questions about who Sivik really was and how he returned from the dead to pass his message on. Was he a messenger from the Gods? If so, what did he mean when he told Tarimev that there would be war?

The stew cooked and Tarimev dug into the bowl with gusto. It was delicious and filled him with warmth. Once the meal was over, he curled up in his bedroll and fell asleep instantly, his dreams full of visions of Sivik's dead eyes staring at him.

14

After an uneventful morning of breakfast, packing up camp and setting off, Tarimev entered the woods that spread into the Yevanti Wilds. The trees were tall and thick, and a dense canopy overhead made it impossible to see more than twenty feet ahead. It was hot under the trees and the further south he travelled, the hotter it would get. For once, Tarimev was pleased that his recruit armour consisted of only a chest plate and leg guards, seeing as wearing full plate mail would be very difficult in this humidity.

The forest floor was covered with brown leaves from the summer's growth, the ground was dry and hard and the undergrowth crowded close to the trunk of each tree as it grew taller. Tarimev had never been this deep into the woods before. He was forever hearing stories of the Wilds, but they all sounded like tales from some other world. He'd heard about the terrible heat, the ferocious animals, and most of all he had heard about the vicious Yevanti Warriors.

They were a strange breed, living deep in the forests at the northern edge of their lands. They wore animal skins and lived by hunting the dangerous beasts roaming these parts. They were said to be uncivilised barbarians who killed anyone they saw outside of their tribe. Tarimev hoped this wasn't true, otherwise, he would have no chance of getting permission to pass through the wilds.

As he passed deeper into the forest, he began to see signs of habitation. The trees thinned out and there were tracks carved into the ground with unlit torches along the way. At last, he saw Qoan, a large wooden city, with spiked wood walls at least twenty feet tall. He prepared to dismount his horse when he heard movement to his right. Just as he looked, an arrow flew out of the undergrowth and landed in his horse's side. The horse reared back and Tarimev lost hold of the reins. Before he could do anything else, the beast bolted away, dragging him behind. He drew his sword and swung it wildly at the stirrup until he managed to cut the leather strap. Then he threw himself out of the way of the horse's rear legs. As the beast rode away, Tarimev rolled clear and scrambled to his feet.

He saw several men dressed in animal skin armour walking towards him. Some of them had bows, while others had spears. He knew he was finished if these were the Yevanti warriors. Instinctively he started to run for the treeline, hoping to evade a painful death. However, as he ran, he heard the sound of running behind him. He looked over his shoulder to see two of the tribesmen chasing him, both carrying small axes.

The Trials of Knights

Tarimev turned again and ran into the forest. He turned to look behind again, then found his foot colliding with a tree root. His leg buckled and he began to fall. He struck his head against a tree, and as his vision faded, thought to himself, "Please Ajo, don't let this be it." The last thing he felt was his body hitting the ground.

After leaving the inn that he spent the night in, Torvald had spent the morning strolling the town, watching people take down the final decorations from the festival. He heard a few mentions of a fight in a tavern, but paid no mind, fights happened every day. He enjoyed a late breakfast at a high-end inn located in the Highscepter Ward, where he had to pay two Zela and ten Sudra for a table. It was worth it though; he ate a huge meal of roast quail, sweet potatoes and rice. He also drank three glasses of wine that cost two Sudra each. When he finally finished eating, he made his way straight to the palace so that he was early for his first duty.

Torvald walked into the main hall and was greeted by a servant who bowed politely and led him through the corridor to the King's throne room. Torvald realised how much he would have to learn about the pomp and ceremony of being a member of the King's knights. While he waited for King Occime, he walked around the hall and stared at the paintings on the wall. He noticed a painting of the King's grandfather, Dumane, standing atop the body of an orc warrior, one hand raised above his head. The picture showed Dumane's sword impaling the orc's torso.

"Its wonderful artwork isn't it." A familiar and

friendly voice said from behind him.

Torvald turned to see the smiling face of Princess Cayte. She looked stunning in her long blue dress, the collar of which was embroidered with silver thread. Her hair was braided loosely at the back with a gold band holding it together. The jewellery she wore was simple and elegant.

"Cayte!" Torvald said, surprised and relieved to see her.

She smiled and held out her hand.

Torvald took her hand and kissed it. Cayte looked around to ensure no-one else was in the room then gave Torvald a kiss on the cheek.

"You look nice today," she said.

"Thank you. I'm glad you like my new clothes."

Torvald was wearing his smartest clothing for once, a neat lilac doublet and grey trousers, yet he still wore his pauldron and sword.

"What brings you here?" Torvald asked.

"Is it not enough for me to miss you?" Cayte said in between laughs. "I thought you might need this." She handed him a large cloth bundle, bound in red ribbon, that clinked as she passed it over, "Don't open that yet. I also wanted to speak to you about Tarimev, to make sure that you were okay."

"What about him? Is he in trouble?"

Cayte shook her head. "You haven't heard? He got into a fight last night, and he killed a man in cold blood."

"What! I should speak to him, where is he?" Torvald was horrified.

"I don't know, he had a secret meeting with my father and Marçhal Bergan this morning. All I know is they sent him on his trial to become a knight. If he succeeds, he will avoid any criminal charges. If he fails … well I hope he doesn't fail."

"I'll go and find him; I've got to help hi-."

Cayte cut him off, "You mustn't. If you abandon your post you will be punished, and if that happened then I wouldn't be able to see you again."

"But Cayte, I can't-"

"Please Torvald, don't worry. Just do your duty, and trust in your friend's skills."

Torvald knew that she was right. If anyone could handle himself it was Tarimev, and besides, he couldn't face not being able to see her again.

"You're right, I'm sure he'll be fine."

Cayte nodded. "I'd better go. My father will be here to see you soon. Take care." She gave Torvald another kiss and left the room.

Torvald stood alone in the room for some time, trying to calm his nerves. He didn't feel right leaving his friend alone on what was likely a dangerous task, but he knew that he had no choice. His thoughts were disturbed by the throne room doors opening and the King entering.

The King was dressed in his usual blue robes with a red cloak. He sat down on his throne and waved his hand, signalling Torvald to come closer. Torvald approached the throne and bowed low.

"Greetings Your Highness," Torvald said.

"It's a pleasure to see you, Sir Storheam," Occime said with a smile, "I trust you are ready to begin your duty as a member of my protectorate?"

Torvald's jaw dropped slightly. To be a part of the King's Protectorate was an honour that usually took years to achieve, and it was unheard of for it to be a first posting. He snapped back into reality and bowed again. "Yes, Your Highness. I am very honoured to take up this position."

"Good, good. Now, you have been chosen to replace Sergeant Galeren after his untimely death. You will now be responsible for defending the royal family. Do you understand?"

"I'm sorry, I don't understand. I am replacing Sergeant Galeren? I thought he was Cay- Princess Cayte's protector," Torvald replied.

"The King's Protectorate is responsible for the defence of the whole Royal Family, and anyone else that I decide for that matter. Galeren was a member of the Protectorate and after his death, my daughter suggested you for the role of her personal guard. It seems you impressed her during your trial at Herfeld. And from what Sergeant Koln told me about you, I think she made a good decision. I can see that she already gave you your armour."

Torvald opened the package Cayte had given him to see that it was the armour of a King's protector, full plate steel armour with golden accents and a base the standard red of Worthervir, all to be topped off with his signature golden pauldron.

"I'm honoured to serve in any position required, Your Highness."

"Wonderful. You will be required to live here in the palace. You will be in Sergeant Galeren's old room, next to the Princess's. She may roam as she pleases within the Palace grounds, but you will be required to escort her wherever she wishes if she leaves. If she is going to an event anywhere in the Kingdom, someone will inform you and you will be required to organise whatever extra protection may be necessary. In addition to that, you will be expected to carry out any tasks I assign you. Are there any questions?"

"No, Your Highness," Torvald answered.

"Very well then, you will join us for dinner tonight. It is customary for any new members of the Protectorate to dine with me and my family during their first duty. After all, it is useful to be friends with the people who will be protecting you. Speak to one of my servants in the entrance hall, they will show you to your room. Your belongings have already been brought over from your previous barracks."

"Thank you, Your Highness."

"My pleasure."

Torvald bowed and left the room, allowing himself to be led away by a servant. When he reached his room, the servant left him and Torvald went inside. The room was extravagantly decorated. In the centre of the room was a four-poster bed, and to the left of the bed was an ornate wooden desk with some writing utensils, a wardrobe, a set of drawers, and a window that overlooked the Grayfalls district and Highscepter ward of the city. The other side of the room had a small dining table, large enough for two or three people to sit with ease, as well as two comfortable chairs with a bookcase in the corner. Torvald walked slowly around the room, taking in everything he could. He got dressed in his new armour and had just poured himself a goblet of wine from a jug that was on the table when there was a knock at the door.

"Come in," Torvald said.

The door opened, and standing on the other side

was Princess Cayte. She walked inside and shut the door behind her.

"I believe you are meant to open the door for a princess, not just say come in."

She giggled at her own joke before walking over to him and giving him a hug.

"I'm so happy they chose you; I didn't know if they would listen to my suggestion," she said.

Torvald smiled as he hugged her back. "I'm glad to be here, Cayte."

They broke apart and looked into each other's eyes. Torvald leaned in to kiss her, but she pulled away quickly, blushing slightly.

"Sorry, I just can't believe how well this is going. If you serve well for a few weeks, we might even be able to tell my parents about us."

Torvald laughed and kissed her again. This time she did not pull away. She kissed him back, pressing her body against his, letting him feel how much he meant to her.

"Come on, I want to go for a walk in the city. It's your job to escort me, is it not?" She said with a smirk.

He laughed and said "Lead the way, Your Majesty. Your wish is my command."

Tarimev's head hurt. His neck felt like it had been snapped and his entire body ached. He groaned and tried to move. Although he was barely conscious, he knew something was wrong. He opened his eyes and saw that he was in some kind of wooden prison cell with wooden bars as a door. He had been stripped of his armour and weapons and was left in his simple brown cloth trousers, white cotton vest tunic, and

The Trials of Knights

plain leather sandals.

"Great. In less than a day I'm in a cell twice," He thought to himself, before realising that if he was in a cell then at least he hadn't been killed. Yet, at least.

As he sat up, his body screamed in pain. But he ignored it for now and concentrated on trying to stand up. The floor was hard and cold, and he moved slowly, testing every muscle in his body. As he stood, he realised that he was being watched. A Yevanti was standing in the doorway, watching him closely.

"You're awake. Eat. You'll meet the Queen soon, trespasser." The guard threw a stale piece of bread through the wooden bars, which landed at Tarimev's feet.

He grunted and picked it up. It tasted awful, but he knew he needed to eat or he would lose strength fast, and he couldn't afford to do that. He chewed slowly, trying to mash the solid bread up enough for him to actually swallow it. After several minutes of eating, he finally finished and the guard said, "That should keep you alive until you see the Queen. Someone will get you later."

With that, the guard left the cell. Tarimev sat down and waited. An hour passed and still no one came. Another hour passed and still he waited. Finally, after another hour had gone by, someone entered the cell. It was another Yevanti soldier, but this time he wasn't armed.

"I am here to take you to see the queen," he said.

Tarimev nodded and got to his feet. He followed the guard out of the cell and into a narrow and dusty corridor. They walked quickly, and before long they went up some stairs into a wooden hall. The floor was covered in straw, and there was a long wooden table in the centre. At one end of the room was an open archway leading to the outside, and at the other end was a carved wooden throne.

Tarimev saw that on the throne was a beautiful woman, not likely more than half a decade older than himself, dressed in leather armour that was trimmed with gold. Her hair was blonde and straight and fell down past her shoulders, and it was held in place with a golden circlet on top of her head. She was wearing a fur trimmed leather cloak, and on her left shoulder was the skull of some sort of horned animal. She was staring directly at Tarimev, her blue eyes piercing into his soul. He was led in front of the throne and the guard saluted, then bowed. The Queen finally spoke.

"Trespasser into our lands, I welcome you to my court. I am Queen Ebbina Meddos, ruler of the Yevanti Tribe."

Tarimev swallowed nervously and took a step forward. "Your Majesty, I mean no harm in your lands. I have been sent to deal with a threat within the mountain to the south. I was travelling here to request your permission to travel your lands, and if possible, be provided with a guide."

Queen Ebbina stared at him for a moment before speaking. "How can we trust such a stranger? What proof do you offer that you are not simply a mercenary who has infiltrated us to steal information?"

Tarimev shook his head. "I cannot prove anything, Your Majesty. All I can tell you is that I have been sent on behalf of the Marçhal Order to defeat this evil."

"The Marçhal Order? I see. Well, that certainly changes things." The Queen turned to one of her guards, "Fetch the ambassador, let's see if he has heard of this evil in the mountain."

15

After spending a lovely afternoon walking around Alerill with Cayte, Torvald finished changing into his nicest clothes and prepared to make his way to the dining hall for his meal with the Royal Family. He had been given an invitation from King Occime himself, one that was not meant to be refused. It would have been nice if he wasn't so nervous as he walked through the halls toward his destination. He was going to have to spend a whole evening across the table from Cayte, whilst pretending that they hadn't started a whole relationship together.

It didn't help matters when he opened his chamber door and saw her standing there. She looked stunning in a deep purple dress with lace sleeves and a high collar. Her long brown hair flowed down over one shoulder in a braid, while she wore light makeup. All in all, she was breathtakingly beautiful.

"Torvald," she said, smiling at him with those big brown eyes of hers. "You look wonderful. I thought it might make a good impression if you escorted me to the dining hall."

He smiled back sheepishly before stepping forward and taking her arm. He knew what she meant about making a good first impression, but he couldn't help but think that this was far too public a setting for them to be alone together. As they stepped out onto the hallway, he spotted several servants and guards staring at them. That only made his heart beat faster and he prayed to all the gods that things went well tonight. They reached the dining hall doors and he knocked on them twice loudly.

The door slid open and he and Cayte stepped inside. The room was large, with a ceiling decorated with crystal chandeliers. A large fireplace sat in the centre of the wall opposite the entrance, with one long table next to it that would seat at least fifty people and had two chairs at the head of the table for the King and Queen. Torvald felt suddenly very small and insignificant, like a child who had stumbled into an adult gathering. The King and Queen were sat at the head of the table, but they both stood up as soon as they saw Torvald and Cayte enter the room.

"Ah, young man!" King Occime exclaimed with a smile. "I'm glad you could join us this evening. Please sit."

Torvald bowed slightly before taking a seat next to the King and opposite Cayte.

"It's a pleasure to be dining with you and your family, Sire," Torvald said with a smile.

Cayte smiled at him, then turned her attention to King Occime. "Thank you for inviting me, Father," she replied.

Occime nodded and gestured for them to eat. Once they had placed their napkins on their laps, multiple servants entered the room carrying platters of food and began serving everyone at the table. There were several types of meat, fish, vegetables and other dishes that Torvald had not seen since he was last in Calramon. During the meal, Torvald made friendly conversation with Cayte, King Occime, and Queen Lorea. He learned that his father and the King had known each other for many years, but it seemed that Occime held Torvald's father in even lower regard than Torvald himself did. At least they had that in common.

"So, how have you found the two years of life in the capital, Torvald?" asked King Occime.

"It's very busy and full of life, Sire. But I am enjoying myself."

King Occime nodded. "That's good to hear. I know it is different to Calramon, but I'm sure there are some similarities. Have you met many people here yet?"

Torvald shook his head. "Only professionally. I've been quite busy with my duties and training."

"Well, I'm sure you will be able to meet many people whilst escorting Cayte to her various events across the kingdom." All had a wonderful evening, and the King and Queen both expressed their gratitude to Torvald for being such an excellent guest. When the meal came to an end, the servants cleared away the plates and glasses from the table. The air of formality had begun to fade away with each glass of wine, and the King was talking with Torvald like they were old friends.

"You know, Torvald. You're a very handsome

young man, and I suspect you'll find plenty of eligible ladies in the city. In fact, there's one sitting across from you right now." Occime laughed as he glanced at Cayte.

Torvald smiled politely. "Oh, I would never be worthy to court your daughter. I'm just a Knight."

"Not just a Knight. You forget that I know your father. You are nobility, and noblemen can marry noblewomen. If you wish to, you could be Cayte's husband." He laughed again as Torvald blushed.

"Father, I think I should probably tell you," Cayte spoke up as she took Torvald's hand, "We are already courting. We have been for a while now."

Occime and Lorea shared a glance, and then without a word, stood up and left the room.

Tarimev had waited in silence for five minutes before Queen Ebbina finally spoke again. "Ah Marçhal, a pleasure to see you. Thank you for coming so quickly. Trespasser, this is Marçhal Ambassador Imre Rein." Tarimev turned to face Imre, who was standing behind him. He was tall, with black hair that was lightly tousled. His features were strong, and he sported a neat goatee. He wore a leather breastplate under a blue and grey overcoat and at his waist was a sword, the crossguard of which was golden, and shaped like the wings of a phoenix, almost identical to that carried by Marçhal Bergan. Except the glowing gem it housed was red. Tarimev stared at Imre in stunned silence before Imre spoke up.

"I can't believe it. Tarimev? Tarimev Riswaell? Is that you?" He walked closer to Tarimev, and Tarimev returned the gesture, then embraced his old friend.

They held each other tightly for a minute or two, before letting go and laughing.

"I don't believe it myself. It's been so long." Tarimev said.

"Indeed, it has. Look at you, a knight."

Tarimev laughed and nodded. "Yes, almost."

Imre looked at him with a smile, and then to Ebbina. "Your Highness, I must apologise for forgoing the proper protocol in greeting you, but I was rather shocked to see this man standing here. He is one of my oldest friends, I have known him since I was born. It has been almost ten years since I last saw him. I am sorry if I have offended you."

Ebbina curtsied gracefully. "There is no need for apologies, dear Ambassador. I understand completely." She looked to Tarimev and back to Imre, "You can vouch for this man then?"

Imre nodded. "Of course. Tarimev is one of the best men I've known my entire life. He sacrificed his childhood to help his father on his farm."

"A friend of yours is a friend of the Yevanti," Ebbina looked at Tarimev, "Mr Riswaell, I will allow you free reign within our lands, and you are free to complete your quest. I will not, however, give you a guide through our lands. Until your people treat us as equals, not barbarians, you will get no aid from us. Marçhal Imre, I believe that you have a spare room in your home, would you allow Mr Riswaell to stay there until he is ready to leave?"

"Of course, he can."

Tarimev bowed low before Ebbina. "Thank you, Your Highness. May I ask, what about my weapons and armour?"

"I will have your armour delivered to the Marçhal later, but you will only have your weapons returned the moment you leave our city." Ebbina stood from her throne, "I hope you enjoy your stay here, Mr Riswaell. Thank you for your time, Marçhal." She turned to leave when Imre said "Your Highness, one more thing." Ebbina turned back to face him once again, "Yes?"

"Your sister was spotted nearby. It seems she has amassed quite a few men."

"How many?"

"Two dozen at least. Enough to give a decent fight to anyone. I think they might even attempt to ambush you."

"Thank you for the information, but Eshami would never dare attack us here. I will have my men find her and her people and put an end to these outcasts."

Imre bowed to the Queen, then looked at Tarimev and nodded his head towards the door. "Come on, old friend. Let's get you somewhere to rest."

Tarimev watched Queen Ebbina leave the room, unable to take his eyes off of her, then followed Imre out of the hall.

The walk to Imre's house was a short one. The house, like most of the buildings in Qoan, was a two-storey wooden building with a thatched roof. Tarimev was shown to his room and left to relax. He bathed using a sponge and water that were in the room, then lay down on the bed for a well-deserved rest.

Torvald and Cayte sat at the table in silence, their eyes fixed on the burning logs in the fireplace. The fire crackled and popped, sending sparks flying into the air.

The Trials of Knights

They stayed still for a while before Cayte finally broke the silence.

"Maybe they weren't ready for our news."

"Why did you tell them? I thought we were keeping it secret still," Torvald snapped.

Cayte looked away from him, casting her gaze down to the floor. "Father seemed to be pushing the idea. I'm sorry, I know you wanted to keep it quiet but it has been six months."

Torvald looked at her for a moment, before looking back to the fire. "They are going to want to discharge me, aren't they?"

Cayte smiled and looked up at him. "No, they won't. I'll make sure of it. I'll talk to them tomorrow morning."

Torvald sighed and leaned forward, resting his elbows on the table. "Thank you. You know, I don't deserve you."

Cayte smiled and turned back to the fire. "You should go to bed; I imagine the King will want to see you in the morning."

"I'm sure he will." Torvald stood, "Goodnight, Cayte."

Torvald walked across the room, stepping out onto the balcony overlooking the courtyard. He watched the moonlight dance over the walls of Alerill, casting shadows on the ground below. When you couldn't see some of the crimes that took place below, the city really was beautiful. As he appreciated the view, Torvald wondered what was to become of his career now. He would probably lose his post. But then again, he had always been good at his job. Hopefully, the King would recognise this and keep him in the military.

Torvald turned and headed back inside, making his way back to his room and quickly undressing. He climbed into the large four-poster bed and closed his eyes, drifting off to sleep almost instantly.

It was early morning when Occime woke up and began to prepare for the day ahead. He made his way to his dressing room, where a servant had already laid out his clothing. He picked up the outfit set on top of the pile and slipped it on, the shirt and trousers fitting perfectly. Once dressed, the King made his way down to the dining hall for breakfast.

The first person he saw was High General Barra, an old elf that had risen through the military ranks, who was at least 240 years old. He still wore his full armour even though he hadn't faced battle since the Orcish Wars ended almost eighty years ago. He kept his white hair and beard neatly trimmed, which was unusual for an elf of his age. He was sitting beside the dining hall entrance, waiting for the King to arrive.

"Good morning, Your Highness," Barra stood and bowed slightly.

"Really, Barra? I haven't even eaten yet." The King chuckled.

Barra shook his head and looked at the floor. "I'm sorry, Your Majesty, I am here on behalf of your daughter."

"Let me guess, you want to talk to me about Sir Storheam?"

"Yes, I'm afraid so. I don't know exactly what he has done, but the princess told me he may be stripped of his position?"

"There is no need to worry, he is not at risk of that. Cayte is overreacting."

"May I ask what it is that Torvald has done?"

"I'm not at liberty to say at the moment, but I will tell you as soon as I can. For now though, old friend, would you be so kind as to fetch Sir Storheam and have him wait in my throne room for me?"

Barra bowed his understanding once more and left the King's side, moving quickly through the servants' quarters. The King sat down at his table and a servant poured him some tea. He sipped at the hot liquid, savouring the taste of it as he waited for his breakfast to be brought in. A few minutes later, two servants entered the dining hall carrying a tray with plates of porridge, fruit and bread. They placed the food down in front of him and left without a word.

As the King began to eat, he was joined at the table by his wife. She looked at her husband and smiled. "Good morning, my love."

King Occime smiled back. "Good morning, my darling."

"You didn't wake me this morning."

"I thought you deserved a rest; you have been working hard lately."

Lorea nodded, "And you have been spending all your time working."

"The kingdom is busy!" Occime laughed, "That makes me busy."

"We must find a way to spend more time together," Lorea said softly.

Occime smiled, "Soon, my love, I promise. I'd better go shortly; Torvald is waiting in the throne room."

"Of course," Lorea got up from her seat and kissed her husband on the cheek. She turned back as she reached the doorway and said "Don't lose your temper. After all, you were young and in love once."

She left the room, leaving Occime alone in his thoughts.

16

Morning in Qoan was much more peaceful than it was in Alerill. There were still people in the streets, but not as many, and not as noisy. Tarimev appreciated this when he awoke from the first good night's sleep in a few days. As he climbed out of bed, he noticed a trunk at the foot of it that hadn't been there when he went to sleep. He opened it up, and found his armour inside it, along with his flintlock pistol. He pondered on why he had been allowed to keep his gun but not his sword or dagger, then decided he would probably find out soon enough. He dressed quickly in his basic garments and then moved to get breakfast downstairs. He found Imre sitting at a small table eating a bowl of porridge, which smelled delicious. "Good morning," said Tarimev.

"Good morning, how are you enjoying the barbarian city?" asked Imre, setting down his spoon.

Tarimev shrugged, "A little better than yesterday."

Imre chuckled, "Glad to hear it. How are your injuries?"

"They're healing nicely. I think they'll be manageable in the next few days, then I'll continue with my quest."

"Glad to hear it. Sit, grab some food."

The two men ate their porridge in silence for several minutes, before Imre spoke again. "So how has life been? I heard bandits attacked Burtop, and that a lot of people died. Is that true?"

Tarimev frowned, "That is true. The bandits killed more people than I'd like to think about, and destroyed a few buildings around town as well... including the farm. That's why I signed up as a knight."

"That's dreadful. How did Cosai cope? He must have been devastated."

"He passed four years before the attack. When the farm burned down, the only thing I had left was his sword," Tarimev paused as he felt tears forming in his eyes. He shook them off, "Anyway, enough about me. How have you been? I'm impressed that you're a Marçhal Ambassador already."

"Thank you, it was pure chance. I got into a bit of trouble when we left Burtop, and I ended up in a street gang. Did petty crimes for a while until we tried our luck at something bigger; we tried to rob the Royal Treasury of Amargond."

"I never heard about any robberies, I'd have thought that sort of news would travel."

"That's because we failed, first person I threatened inside happened to be the Marçhal Blademaster himself. I was young and stupid so I tried to fight him. He obviously won, but he was impressed by my courage and offered to take me to the Marçhal Citadel to make something of myself. Five years later, I was adept at magic and qualified for my first placement as a Marçhal. I was sent here to try and bring the Yevanti away from their barbarian ways. Once I arrived, I discovered that the myths of the Yevanti weren't anything like reality. When I reported back to the Grandmaster, he decided that the Yevanti should be treated as any other realm, and I was made the official Marçhal Ambassador to the Yevanti. It's a shame though, even others in my order still believe the lies concocted about this tribe."

Tarimev nodded, "I've heard those rumours. To be honest, I was terrified to come here. I thought I'd be skinned and eaten or something, but I'm glad I came."

"If you need help with anything, just ask. I have to go now, I have a meeting with Queen Meddos in an hour." Imre stood from his chair and pulled his coat from the back of his chair.

"You and the Queen seemed very friendly, is there something there?"

Imre laughed at his friend's implication, "She's a great woman, beautiful too. She has a lot of qualities that you don't see in most leaders, cares deeply for her people, and isn't afraid to get her hands dirty." Tarimev felt an unexpected pang of jealousy as Imre extolled the virtues of the Yevanti Queen, "but no, I'm a married man."

"You're married?"

"Yes, almost five years now. Her name is Jarea, we met in Askerskali. Now she's back at the Citadel." Imre paused at the door for a moment, "I'll be back around midday; would you want to meet up for lunch? There's a wonderful drinking hall on the south side of the city."

"Sure, sounds good. Looking forward to it."

Tarimev watched as Imre walked out of the room and closed the door behind him, leaving the morning sun shining through the window. He sighed. He wanted to leave today, he didn't know how long he could stand to stay in this place, not while his quest was unfinished. Yet, he knew that if he was to try to face a necromancer with his current injuries, he wouldn't stand a chance.

For half an hour, Torvald waited in the Throne Room. His stomach was churning. if it wasn't bad enough that he had been summoned by the King, he was awoken by the highest-ranking man in the whole army, High General Barra himself. A man second only to King Occime when it came to military influence in Worthervir. Every possible scenario of what might happen when Occime entered the room flooded his mind. Would he be discharged from his position? Imprisoned for treason? Banished from the kingdom? Whatever happened, he was certain that the King was furious, otherwise, he wouldn't have left without a word the previous night.

Occime entered the room, looking haggard and worn. He sat down heavily on his throne, motioning for Torvald to stand opposite. Torvald took his place and bowed to the King.

"I trust you know why you are standing before me?" Occime asked.

"I do, Your Highness, "Torvald said.

"Very well then, let us speak plainly. I was shocked after what Cayte told me last night." He paused for a moment, allowing the words to sink in. "But I am more shocked by you, Torvald. By the fact that you went ahead to pursue this relationship with her."

"With respect, Majesty, if you are expecting me to apologise, I will not. I love your daughter, and she loves me. Relieve me of my post if you wish, but it will not change how I feel."

"I will be honest with you, Torvald, I did suspect that Cayte might have been interested in you when she requested you as her personal guard. However, I didn't think that something was already going on between you when I appointed you to the position. No, I was truly surprised last night. That is why I sent for you this morning. You will be pleased to hear that I am not relieving you of your position. After all, who will protect my daughter more than the man that loves her."

Torvald breathed a sigh of relief. "Thank you, Majesty."

"However, I expect you to be discreet about your feelings towards my daughter. This is not to become public until I say so, and you should be aware that I am only allowing this because of your father's standing."

"Of course, Majesty."

"Good. Now go and wake my daughter. After you do, I want you to find out what happened last night, some guards were found in the grounds with their throats slit and armour taken."

Torvald bowed to Occime and left the room. As

soon as the door shut behind him, he broke into a run, heading straight for Cayte's quarters. He knocked on the door, then pushed it open, "Cayte!" he shouted with joy.

Inside the room, he saw the room was a mess, like a struggle had taken place, and a letter was on the Princess's bed sitting atop a pile of brown fibres. He grabbed it and read the contents. It was a letter that read:

King Occime,

I have your daughter. I expect to be brought 400 Linya in Sosek village three days from now. If not, your daughter will be returned to you piece by piece. I trust you will make the right choice. I hope you can tell from her hair, that we are being serious.

The Pirate King.

Torvald fell to the floor, tears streaming down his cheeks. "Oh Cayte," he sobbed as his mind ran away from him thinking the worst of what may happen to his love.

He picked himself up off the ground and dashed down the corridors, running back toward the Throne Room. He burst inside, gasping for breath.

"Your Grace," Torvald gasped, his eyes still red and wet. "Cayte has been kidnapped."

"By whom?" Occime asked, his voice cold.

"A man claiming to be 'the Pirate King' has her, and he expects payment in Sosek village in three days' time." He showed the King the letter he found on the bed.

"This can't be true!" Occime spat, his eyes

widening. "How dare he attack in my own home!" he roared with fury in his voice. He fell back into his throne and rubbed his face.

"What do you want to do, Majesty?" Torvald asked.

"We must find the Pirate King and destroy him. I don't care how much he wants money; we will not allow that." Occime turned to one of his guards, "Fetch the Marçhal and the High General, bring them to the war room immediately. Do not tell them what has happened yet." The guard nodded and left the room, taking his orders and rushing to comply.

"Come with me, Torvald," Occime ordered. Together they went through the castle, towards the war room.

Once Tarimev had finished his breakfast, he went out to explore the city of Qoan. For the first time since he had joined the King's army, he left without wearing any of his armour, the only thing he carried was his flintlock attached to the back of his belt. He felt safer in the so-called 'barbarian city' than he ever had in Worthervir.

He walked around the market, purchasing some drinking water and trinkets from a vendor. He was approached by a woman selling fruit, who offered him a free sample. He accepted and found the fruit sweeter than anything he had tasted before. He purchased a bag of the fruit and continued walking. Soon enough, he came across an old man sitting on a bench and reading a book. He sat beside the man and watched the world for a moment, enjoying the peace and quiet.

After a few minutes, the man looked up from his book and smiled at Tarimev. "Hello there," he said, making conversation with Tarimev. "Where are you off to today?"

"I'm just exploring the city. Where are you from?"

"Originally, I lived in Drotabi, but I moved here with the rest of the tribe when the last King united everyone. What about you? Which tribe are you from?"

"Oh, I'm not from a tribe, I'm from Worthervir. My name is Tarimev, what's yours?"

"My name is Raimas. Nice to meet you, Tarimev."

"Likewise, Raimas. I've got to say, I'm surprised by this town. I was always taught that the Yevanti were something to fear. When I see all these people living together like they're one big family, I wonder why I was ever told that."

"Well, we're not as bad as you might think," Raimas chuckled. "Don't get me wrong, generations ago we were, but Queen Ebbina changed all of that. The Last King managed to bring us all together, and he made sure that nobody would take advantage of the tribes again."

"It's a shame that the world doesn't know this. If they did, perhaps your people would be more accepted."

Raimas looked at him kindly and placed his hand on his shoulder. "The world needs an enemy Tarimev, even in times of peace. People are more comfortable thinking that there are dangers out there to keep them feeling safe. The Elves, Cascurans, Dwarves and Nargonds have pirates. Unfortunately, the Amargondians and the Worthervirians have chosen us. It's not perfect, but it works. It keeps outsiders from our lands."

"Perhaps. But would you not prefer your people to be united with the world?"

"Of course, I would, we all would. It won't happen though, not until the world has another enemy to focus on." Raimas stood up and stretched his arms. "Nice meeting you Tarimev, I hope you enjoy your time in our city."

Tarimev stood up too and gave a smile of thanks. He walked down the street and continued exploring. He saw the sun reaching its peak in the sky, and so began walking south to try and find the drinking hall that Imre told him about. He passed many shops, taverns and houses along the way. Children ran by him in the street, laughing and playing with each other. Families sat outside their houses, chatting away to each other. There were no soldiers or knights in sight, just normal people living their lives as they pleased. This was the true nature of the Yevanti people, he thought to himself. They didn't care about war, they didn't care about the politics between different kingdoms, they only cared about living their own lives. This was the life, he thought to himself.

After some time, he reached a square by the south wall of the city. In the centre of it was a large drinking hall, with several tables and chairs scattered around outside. The front of the wooden building was open to the sun, giving it a warm feel. A group of people stood at the bar, talking amongst themselves.

Tarimev looked inside and saw Imre sitting at a table with two large mugs on it. He went and sat opposite his friend.

"Afternoon, Tarimev!" Imre greeted him cheerfully. "Did you find the place ok?"

"Yes, thank you. Is this for me?" He said picking up the mug that was still full.

"Indeed, it is. Yevanti Ale. Stronger than anything you'll get back home, and sweeter than nectar. It's a taste that will stay with you long after you've left."

"Sounds good to me." Tarimev had a swig from the mug and let out a sigh of relief.

"If you want anything to eat, there is a boar on the spit in the back room."

"No, no food. I'm fine," Tarimev said, taking another drink.

"You're going to get drunk on the first day," Imre laughed.

"Well, I have nowhere to be."

Imre rolled his eyes "All right, if you insist," He paused to take a sip of his ale, "So, what do you think of Qoan?"

Tarimev took a moment to consider how best to answer. "I suppose I'm surprised to see such a friendly town; what with all those stories I've been told about the Yevanti."

"Ah yes, the tales of the terrifying warriors who live in the wilds, I remember them. Well, they may seem scary but, as I'm sure you've noticed, they are also kind, hard-working and generous. The people of Qoan understand their place in the world, they don't need to prove themselves in anyone else's eyes. It's refreshing."

The two men got some food while they continued talking for almost an hour before Imre stood up. "I'd better head off now, I'm leading a scouting party to try and find the outcasts. I'll be gone for a day or two. Enjoy yourself, I'm sure I'll see you again before you leave."

He shook Tarimev's hand and left the drinking hall. Tarimev finished his drink, then took his leave.

Occime and Torvald walked in silence through the castle, the only noises they heard was the clinking of armour as guards saluted the king. Finally, they reached the war room and walked inside. The war room was dark, the walls bare stone and the only form of illumination a chandelier casting light on a rectangular table upon which was a map of the known world.

Upon entering, the two men inside stood to attention

"Your Majesty," they said in unison.

Occime looked at them and smiled. "Good morning, both of you."

They bowed their heads in return. Occime signalled for them to take a seat, and the two men sat. Occime turned to Torvald and said "This is your job. Brief them."

Torvald cleared his throat and began speaking.

"Marçhal Bergan, High General Barra, thank you for coming so quickly." Torvald began, addressing the two men. "There's been an attack in the palace. Princess Cayte has been kidnapped by pirates."

Both men were shocked into silence.

"Do we know how she is?" Bergan asked, barely able to contain his emotions.

"As far as we are aware, the only thing they have done to her so far is cut her hair as some kind of warning. From the letter I found, we believe she is still alive."

Both the High General and the Marçhal breathed

sighs of relief, their shoulders drooping slightly. Torvald continued reading the letter from the Pirate King to the two men. Once he had finished, he took his seat at the table and awaited questions. The four men sat in silence for a few moments. Then, Barra spoke.

"When do we ride north? It takes three days to get to Sosek, maybe four, depending on the weather further north."

"We don't go," Occime said, standing. "Torvald is going alone. We will send ravens to every outpost on the way to have a new horse ready for him. He can be in Sosek before tomorrow evening if he leaves soon. If he takes men then he will be slowed down by the convoys."

"Might I make a suggestion, Your Majesty?" Barra asked, rising to his feet.

"Make it quick."

"My cousin is a Captain in the Elven navy. He specialises in hunting pirates, and I received word from him two days ago that he is currently docked in Magrin making repairs. I could send word for him to be prepared to accompany Torvald when he arrives. It would speed things up considerably."

"I like the idea very much," Occime agreed. "Send the word and tell Torvald where to meet your cousin. Torvald, prepare a horse, you must leave within the hour."

Torvald rose and nodded; he left without saying goodbye to any of the men. He walked out of the war room and made his way down towards the stables.

17

Tarimev's second day in Qoan started just as his first. A nice quiet breakfast, followed by a stroll through the city streets. Again, he left his armour behind and only carried his pistol with him, still unsure why the Yevanti had let him keep it when they kept his other weapons. As he walked through the marketplace, Tarimev observed how different their world was to his own. The people of Qoan appeared happy and well fed, their children clean and healthy. He finished his walk through the marketplace and went to the same drinking hall where he had lunch with Imre the day before. It was almost entirely empty today, but there were two Yevanti guards sat outside with drinks. Inside, there was nobody except an old lady behind the bar who looked at Tarimev and gave him a friendly smile.

"Welcome back, Visitor," she said. "What will you

have?"

Tarimev smiled. "The same as yesterday."

She nodded and picked up a mug from behind the counter. "You're welcome to sit down," she said, pointing towards a couple of chairs. She returned to her task of preparing the drink for Tarimev, when he spoke up again.

"Quiet in here today. Where is everyone?"

"Most of the men here usually are off-duty scouts and hunters, and they have been sent into the Wilds to find the Queen's sister. I hope they find her, that girl was always trouble."

"I heard that she leads some outcasts?"

"Criminals. They were expelled from the various tribes over generations. When the last King chose his youngest daughter, Ebbina, to succeed as Queen, her sister rebelled. Eshami tried to kill the Queen on the day of her crowning. She was supposed to bow to the new Queen, but instead she tried to stab her. The last King stepped in the way, taking the blade to his chest. The guards seized her and Queen Ebbina had to choose how to punish her sister. She was only seventeen, she wasn't ready for that sort of decision. So she sent her away to the outcasts. Poor girl, she was only a child and she lost her whole family in a day."

She handed the drink to Tarimev who thanked her. It tasted exactly the same as yesterday – sweet and warm. As he sipped the drink, the old woman came around and placed a small plate of food in front of him, along with a large bowl of water.

"Thank you." He smiled at her. "How much?"

She bowed her head slightly. "No charge. Marçhal Imre is paid for by the Queen, and that extends to his friends."

As Tarimev ate his meal, the city started to get louder. As he ate the last bite of what he assumed was boar; bells began to ring throughout the city.

"You must hide, quickly." The old woman shouted, running towards him. "We are being attacked."

He had been riding non-stop for a day now, so when Magrin was on the horizon Torvald kicked his horse into a final gallop. He felt like he had been on the saddle forever. His legs ached, his back hurt and his eyes were bleary from lack of sleep. But even tired, he knew that if he didn't reach her soon, the Princess would be in serious danger.

He reached the town border just after sunrise and rode directly to the town's port. There was nobody about; the sailors were still sleeping and the dockworkers were just waking. He dismounted and tied his horse to a post next to another horse. He walked down the rows of ships, looking at all of the names until he saw it. His heart leaped as he read it aloud; 'Ayverin'. It was a beautiful ship, a frigate, the hull painted the deep green of the elves. Flying atop the highest mast was the flag of Forlerin: a white horse with a red mane on a background of the same green as the ship.

He walked up the gangplank onto an empty deck and knocked on the door of the captain's cabin. The door opened and a young elf stood before him, not much older than fifty years of age, wearing a Forlerian Captain's uniform.

"You must be Sir Torvald Storheam?" The elf asked.

"I am. Captain Wilek, I presume?"

Wilek nodded and gestured for him to enter. "Please come in, Sir Torvald."

Torvald stepped inside and found himself in a room decorated with golden frames holding numerous portraits of the elven royal family. In the centre of the room was an ornate desk, carved from cherry wood. The Captain took his seat and gestured to the opposite one. "Would you care for something to eat or drink, Sir Torvald? You look worn out."

"Thank you, but no. I've ridden hard, haven't slept, and this is the first time I have sat down since I left Alerill but we should get to business. I am on a time sensitive mission. How much have you been told?"

The Captain nodded. "Not much, my cousin's letter only said you had a pirate problem."

"That's right, Captain. The princess of Worthervir has been kidnapped by the Pirate King, and he wants to exchange her for 400 Linya. I have two more days to meet him at Sosek before he starts mutilating her. If I don't make it, she dies."

Wilek nodded. "Well, pirates are my expertise. I will wake my men, we will set sail before noon. With the wind as it is, we will be there by dusk." He began to stand up.

"No. We cannot sail. He will most likely flee if he sees a naval ship. I was hoping you would travel with me by land. If we take horses we will arrive in the late afternoon. We will be able to assess the situation and hopefully extract the Princess without any harm coming to her."

"Of course. This is your mission, I will take your lead. Allow me some time to prepare, I will meet you

The Trials of Knights

on the town outskirts shortly."

Torvald nodded. "Thank you, Captain."

Torvald stood and left the cabin. He returned to his horse and made his way to the edge of town. He checked his weapons and horse gear one last time and then sat to wait for Captain Wilek.

Around the table of Worthervir's war room was the full Worthervirian Military Council. All five men, and the king, were discussing how to deal with the pirate issue. Whilst the men argued amongst themselves, Occime stood from his chair and shouted "We must prepare a counter-attack. This is an attack on me, on my family, on my people, and on my whole kingdom." His voice trembled with emotion.

Captain Roskin cleared his throat, "Sire, our navy is not enough to take on all of the pirates. Our military focuses on land warfare, you know this."

"That might be, Provel, but we are more organised than the pirates," Admiral Larstope countered. "It is also true that we do not have a great deal of ships available, but we can send word to the Elves and the Dwarves. They will be willing to lend us their navy."

Occime looked at the world's map on the table in front of him and studied the distance between the Dwarven lands of the Halled Mountains and his own lands. In his head he calculated the time it would take to the Dwarves to travel to Alerill. He knew they would have to delay any mobilisation of troops until an envoy could make it to the Halled Mountains and return with the Dwarven Navy. He spoke to his council and addressed such a point.

The men looked at each other, none wanting to

The Trials of Knights

volunteer for such a task.

"Might I make a suggestion, Your Majesty?" Sergeant Koln asked.

"Yes, Talbot?"

"We cannot make any moves against the Free Islands until Sir Storheam returns with Princess Cayte. With that in mind, and knowing how exceptional the young man has been so far, might we send him to the Dwarves upon his return?"

All eyes turned to the sergeant. "Forgive me if I am wrong, but what makes you all think they will help?" asked Marçhal Bergan.

High General Barra smiled, "They were our allies during the Orcish war and we have not wronged them since. I am sure they will be happy to send aid."

"As a veteran yourself, Barra, you are well aware that the Orcish wars ended seventy-seven years ago. This kingdom has had very little diplomatic relations with the dwarves since. So, I ask again, why should they help us?"

"It is in both our interests for the pirates to be dealt with quickly. I hear that the dwarves have had some trouble exporting their metals due to pirate attacks," argued Admiral Larstope.

"You are forgetting one thing," Captain Roskin interjected. "If the Dwarves agree to help us, they will expect a reward. Even if it benefits them, they will do nothing for free. Such a reward may be beyond the realms of what we can afford."

"I believe that such a gift will be worth it," said Koln.

"The Sergeant is right. If we manage to stop the pirates, we will have a greater reputation and prestige in the world. Without attacks on our merchant ships, our economy will grow, and having led the destruction of these rogues we will be respected throughout th-"

"Enough!" the King yelled, cutting him off, "The only thing we seem to have agreed on is that whatever action we should take should wait until the Princess is returned safely. In that respect, I am calling an end to this meeting. We shall wait until Torvald returns before we take any further action."

The roars of battle rang out throughout Qoan, and these were sounds that Tarimev couldn't ignore. He left the back room that he was hiding in and took off towards the noises. Soon he found himself on the edge of a fight between many Yevanti, both men and women. Each faction was indiscernible from the other in his eyes, but not to them. Thankfully, he saw one man engaged in a battle that he recognised, the man who brought food to his cell. Tarimev rushed to his aid, intending to tackle the man he was in combat with. As soon as he broke into a sprint, the injuries from days before began to flare up, but the pain spurred him on. As mental as they were physical, they reminded him of the pain that landed him in Qoan in the first place, and his duty to avoid that again. He neared the two men and leaped into the air.

The man he tackled was taken off guard by his sudden arrival and fell back onto the ground, dropping his axe as he fell. Tarimev grabbed the man's neck, and squeezed with all his might, forcing his own weight down on top of him. As the outcast began to lose consciousness, the Yevanti he was fighting struck down with his wooden mace. It slammed into the man's skull, bursting blood and viscera onto the floor. The Yevanti Jailor lifted Tarimev to his feet and handed him the handaxe that the outcast had dropped.

"Thank you," Tarimev muttered.

"Thank you, trespasser," replied the Jailor. "Now go. They will kill everyone."

Tarimev nodded and turned away. A few paces later he heard a scream, and spun around to see the Jailor's body lying face down on the ground. Standing over him was another Yevanti, clutching a blood-soaked battleaxe. The outcast let out a battle cry and charged at Tarimev. The outcast swung his axe wildly, trying to catch Tarimev unaware, but he was prepared and dodged each strike. The outcast was strong for his size, but he had no training in the art of combat. Tarimev waited patiently for the moment to strike, and just as the outcast raised his axe to swing down, Tarimev stepped forward and caught the axe's handle with his free hand. He swung his weapon at the enemy and made contact with his stomach, sending the outcast stumbling backwards as he clutched his stomach to try and keep his insides together. Blood poured through his fingers and the outcast collapsed to the ground, crying for mercy. Tarimev stopped short of killing him and looked around, seeing that the fight around him had thinned. The invasion was spreading into the city, and with Imre and most of the Yevanti Warriors out of the city, there was no one to protect the Queen. If these outcasts killed her and captured the city, they would surely kill him as well.

Tarimev slipped his axe into his belt and ran through the streets of the city. He could hear the sounds of screams and wailing coming from everywhere he went. There was panic around him, and he felt it too, but he knew what he had to do. He passed many fights on his way, and the dust rising from the roads made it hard to see. It felt like a lifetime of running, his head pounding in agony; but it was, in reality, mere minutes before he arrived at the Queen's Great Hall. He glanced around nervously before running up the steps and entering the hall. Near the throne at the far end of the room Ebbina was kneeling, her face bruised and arms bound. Behind her was a woman; similar in looks and age to Ebbina, but not as beautiful in Tarimev's eyes. He realised that she must be Eshami, the Queen's sister, leader of the Yevanti Outcasts. She held a dagger in her hand, while a large group of Outcasts stood in the audience area of the hall, cheering her on. Eshami raised her knife to quiet her people.

"My warriors," she shouted with an air of superiority. "We have finally claimed our prize after generations of waiting."

Her people cheered.

"Our raid has been a success. We have taken Qoan and the Queen herself. These people who declared us criminals, outcasts, even traitors, are now our slaves. Now, join me, in my first execution as Queen of the Yevanti, the death of Ebbina Meddos. THE FALSE QUEEN!"

The crowd roared their approval, their voices echoing across the walls of the great hall.

Ebbina's face drained white as she was dragged to her feet by Eshami. Her expression remained stoic, even as the blade was pressed to her throat and a single bead of blood ran down her neck.

"Stop!" Tarimev bellowed, and the Outcasts turned to look at him. All eyes were fixed on him. Eshami pushed her sister aside, and Ebbina fell back to the floor. She raised her dagger and pointed it towards Tarimev.

"You dare to interrupt me? Are you mad? Are you stupid enough to think that I will allow this insolence? You are not even Yevanti."

Tarimev reached behind his back and drew his flintlock from its holster. He pointed it towards Eshami and drew back the hammer with his left hand.

"I am a knight of Worthervir," said Tarimev, his voice calm yet deadly serious. "For what you have done to these people and their Queen, I will kill you. I suggest you allow it to be quick."

Eshami laughed, "Kill me. How to you expect to get past all of my warriors without being cut down?"

He noticed that the outcasts were making their way to him, weapons in hand, and he understood why he was allowed to keep his pistol. The Yevanti had never seen one before. In their eyes, his only weapon was his axe, and he would only be a threat up close. He smiled a small smile when he thought how wrong they were. He adjusted his hand to ensure his aim was true, and pulled the trigger.

His bullet hit Eshami in the chest, ripping through her leather armour, and she staggered backwards, before falling to her knees. The outcasts rushed him and he had just enough time to drop the gun and draw his axe before they reached him. He blocked a first blow and brought his axe around to strike the outcast in the leg. He spun away from another attack and struck out with his other arm, catching an outcast in the groin and dropping him to the ground. He took another swing at his attackers but misjudged his strike, and a metal mace collided with his ribs. He doubled over in pain as the wind was knocked from his lungs, and he prepared to feel a final blow against him, when a rally cry was heard from outside the hall. A number of Yevanti charged inwards, led by Marçhal Rein, and Tarimev breathed a sigh of relief as he saw them. They fought well, and the Outcasts were soon pushed back from Tarimev.

They retreated out of the hall and fought on the stone steps. Tarimev ignored his injuries again, dropped his axe, and ran to help Queen Ebbina. She was still alive, but barely conscious. Her head was bleeding badly, and she was clearly in a great deal of pain. He took the dagger from Eshami's corpse and cut through the Queen's bindings.

"Can you walk?" he asked.

She nodded.

"Come with me," he said, picking her up and putting her arm around his shoulder. "Imre is holding off the Outcasts for now."

Ebbina pointed to a door behind the throne.

"That way," she said.

Tarimev opened the door into what was obviously her living quarters. There was no fancy furniture, or any expensive comfort that would be found in any other Queen's living quarters. There were simply two rooms, separated by an archway. One room had a bed with two trunks at the foot of it and an armour stand to the side, while the other had three cupboards and a small dining table with four chairs. All the furniture was wooden, just like the floor and walls. He placed

Ebbina gently on the bed and went to rummage through a cupboard. He came up with a bottle of brown liquid and two wooden cups. He pulled the cork from the bottle and took a sniff. It smelled strongly of spices and alcohol - he would recognise the scent of brandy anywhere. He poured some of it into each of the cups, then handed one to Ebbina.

"Drink this. It'll ease your pain."

She drank, grimacing as the liquor burned going down.

"Why did you do this?" she asked.

"What?"

"Kill Eshami. You have no reason to, you could have fled, left Qoan and finished your quest."

"I know," he said with a reassuring smile, "but I couldn't leave your people here to suffer under Eshami's rule. I certainly couldn't allow her to kill you. That would be a waste of such beauty."

She smiled weakly at him, "Thank you, my saviour."

Tarimev finished his drink and poured the two of them another glass. The adrenaline of the fight, combined with the brandy, made him feel very relaxed. He leaned forwards and placed his hand under her chin, bringing her face closer to his own. He moved his lips to hers and kissed her softly. Her kiss was sweet yet familiar, and in the instant their lips touched, he felt a sudden sense of peace come over him. For a moment, Ebbina started to lean into the kiss, but then stopped herself and withdrew her head back. She looked at him, her eyes filled with sadness.

"What is it?" he asked.

"Nothing," she said. "We shouldn't have done that. I'm sorry. It's just too soon."

Tarimev tried to hide his disappointment, but she could see right through him.

"It's fine," he said, stepping away from the bed. "I understand. You should rest, I'll see how Imre is doing."

He walked out of the room, internally berating himself for daring to make a move on the Queen of the Yevanti. As he opened the door to the other room, he saw Imre standing outside, looking back towards the main hall.

"Since you're back in here," Tarimev said. "I take it we've won?"

Imre nodded, "All of the outcasts are either dead or fleeing. Are you alright? And Queen Ebbina?"

"Yes, she's a strong woman. She is resting now, and I think I should do the same. I'll see you back at home."

"You might want this back," Imre said, handing him back his pistol, "Make sure you don't rest too long. After a win like this, the tribe will have a feast to celebrate. You should be there."

Tarimev nodded and walked towards the exit. His mind was whirling with thoughts of what had happened. He knew that he needed to stay focused on his mission, and not get distracted by emotion. He had done it again, just like when he was younger: fallen in love with the idea of a woman rather than the woman herself. But he couldn't stop thinking about Ebbina, and wondering whether he had lost his chance to court her favour.

18

Torvald and Captain Artemus Wilek rode along the north coast of Worthervir in silence. The sun was low on the horizon, its light yellowing the sea a dull orange. They broke away from the coast when the masts of a ship could be seen over the crest of the next hill. They were about to reach their destination.

They rode up a hill where they would be able to see the village of Sosek in its entirety, as well as the docks on the northern side of the bay. Aside from small, two-man fishing boats, the only ship in the docks was a ship with an entirely black hull and dark green sails.

"That's the Pirate King's ship," Torvald said. "The Golden Phoenix." He turned to look at Captain Wilek who was drawing a spyglass from his belt. "Not as grand as I expected," he added.

Wilek looked through the glass for several minutes before lowering it, "Something's not right. I always heard that The Golden Phoenix was trimmed with

The Trials of Knights

gold, and why would the Pirate King not be flying his flag?" he asked, holding the glass up so Torvald could look through it. It showed them a ship flying the flag of a generic pirate, a single skull, flown only by pirates who hadn't earned their name.

"I don't know," Torvald replied. He handed the spyglass back to Wilek, "Can you see the king?"

Captain Wilek peered into the glass once more, then shook his head. "No, but there are two men in the middle of the village. They look like pirates, and everyone else looks to be a villager."

Torvald frowned and dismounted his horse. He led it over to a nearby tree and tied it up. "We should approach on foot." He drew his sword as he walked down the hill towards the village, with Wilek swiftly following him.

They walked into the village square and Torvald called out, "Hello! We're here to meet with the Pirate King."

The two men standing near the docks didn't respond, and neither did the villagers in the streets lining each side of the road.

"What is going on here?" Torvald demanded, "Why aren't you answering me? Your King is expecting me."

The two men glanced at one another before turning back to Torvald. Both had long moustaches, white as the rest of their skin, and both had short swords hanging from their belts. One of them spoke, "Who are you?"

"My name is Sir Torvald Storheam, Knight of Worthervir and Protector of Princess Cayte Sunovren. This is my companion Captain Artemus Wilek, we have business with the Pirate King."

The man with the shorter moustache scoffed, "Well you didn't do a very good job did you. Wait here, I'll fetch the captain."

He turned and started walking down the street while the other man stepped forward.

"Have you the money?" he asked.

Torvald nodded, "That's not your business. I will deal with the Pirate King, nobody else."

The man drew his sword and pointed it at Torvald. "Then let us hope you're better than the last knight I met, or I may cut off your head myself."

A shout came from a building nearby, "Enough!"

The pirate stopped and looked, as did Torvald, and saw that the shouting had come from an old man standing in the doorway of a tavern. He appeared to be in his fifties, dressed in a smart leather waistcoat atop a red tunic with a gold-handled naval hanger at his waist. His head was covered by a wide-brimmed leather hat, tipped downwards to conceal most of his face. From what little of his head could be seen, it was clear that he was bald and sporting grey mutton chops that were connected by his moustache. Yet his most distinctive feature was the dull gold hook in place of his left hand.

"I am Captain Daykon Edmonds of the Free Islands, otherwise known as the Pirate King," he announced, stepping into the town square. The pirate in front of Torvald moved to stand aside, letting Daykon take his place. The Pirate King looked at Torvald and Wilek and nodded to himself, "Well it seems you've made it in time."

Captain Wilek leaned into Torvald and whispered, "His hook should be gold, I've always heard he takes great pride in keeping it polished, and the base should be adorned with gems."

"Care to share with us all, Artemus?" Daykon asked, in a sarcastic tone.

"We want to see the Princess," Torvald said, putting on his most powerful sounding voice, "And we mean to see her now."

Daykon stared at Torvald for a few seconds, then nodded, "Fine, but you will wait here." He turned and headed towards the tavern.

Now that they were alone, Captain Wilek spoke up again, "Sir Storheam, this cannot be the Pirate King. Nothing seems to add up. There is no flag, very few pirates, and his hook doesn't match the rumours."

"As long as he has the Princess, it doesn't matter," Torvald replied. "We focus on keeping her safe."

Wilek sighed, "Of course."

Wilek and Torvald waited until the Pirate King returned, this time accompanied by two others. The two had swords at their hips and carried pistols holstered on their waists. Behind them, bound in chains, barefoot and wearing cloth wraps, was Princess Cayte. She was beaten and bruised. Her hair was short, barely below her ears, and roughly cut as though done with a blunt knife. Tears ran freely down her cheeks as she sobbed uncontrollably. But even through her sobs she smiled slightly when she saw Torvald was there for her.

Daykon stopped in front of Torvald again, and dragged the Princess to his side, "Now then, where's my money?"

After a well-earned rest, Tarimev awoke, sore from his fights but otherwise fine. He rose to see the sun beginning to set on the Yevanti horizon. He remembered what Imre had told him earlier concerning the feast, and so he got dressed in his clothes, even donning his armour in an attempt to look more formal. As he walked out from the house, he could hear the sound of laughter and music. It sounded like people dancing. It was coming from the direction of the great hall. He followed the noise and found his guess to be correct, it seemed like the entire tribe had gathered to dance and drink as one. He watched for a few minutes before a voice shouted his name.

"Tarimev!" Imre called, staggering towards him. "Come join us, we have many a tale to tell tonight, and you must hear them! Come!"

Imre grabbed Tarimev's arm and pulled him along. He seemed very drunk, and he stumbled towards the hall with Tarimev in tow. Once inside, the sounds of revelry grew louder. Tarimev noticed that the tables had been pushed aside to make space for a large fire pit, and Queen Ebbina was sat atop her throne with a cup in her hand. She looked much better than when he left her, she was well-rested and had cleaned off the grime of battle. Beside her stood the tallest member of the tribe, a man who bore a striking resemblance to the Queen. Both were clad in similar leather armour, but the Queen's was decorated with intricate patterns.

Queen Ebbina noticed Tarimev and stood from her throne, "Saviour! Come here, I wish to thank you for saving our lives."

Tarimev made his way in front of the Queen, knelt down on one knee and bowed his head slightly, "Your Majesty. I am glad you're safe."

She gently placed her hand on his cheek, "You needn't bow to me. Stand."

He stood and faced her. She looked around the room, then back to Tarimev, "I wish to honour you, Sir Tarimev."

"Thank you, but it is not Sir, I am simply a trainee."

"In that case, I wish to honour you, Yevan Tarimev."

A small cheer went up from the crowd. Tarimev looked to Imre, who whispered to him, "To be named Yevan is a great honour, it is a name passed down from the founder of the Yevanti to only the worthiest of the title. Only people who have gone beyond what is expected can be granted the title. Each King or Queen can only bestow the title once in their reign. It makes you honorary nobility of the tribe. You should be proud of your new title."

Ebbina spoke again, "In honour of your new title, I grant you this token of my esteem." She handed him a wooden box, which he opened to find a pauldron, fashioned from silver with gold trimming around the edges, in the shape of a lion's head. "This was my great-great-grandfather's. It has been passed down from him and the last person to wear it was my father."

Tarimev nodded, "Thank you Your Majesty, I am honoured to be given such a gift."

"With this pauldron, you are an honorary member of the Yevanti Tribe." She motioned towards his current pauldron, "May I?"

Tarimev nodded and turned to the side, allowing her remove his old pauldron and replace it with the new one. She did so without saying a word, and when she finished, he lowered his arms.

The Queen raised her cup and shouted, "We welcome to the tribe Yevan Tarimev, the Saviour of Qoan."

The Yevanti Tribe roared their approval, and Tarimev could feel his heart soar at the praise, but he was still unsure how to respond. Then Imre stepped forward, "Do not feel pressured to speak, Yevan. You have done enough already by saving the Queen."

Ebbina smiled and spoke, "Let us toast to Yevan Tarimev, the Saviour of Qoan."

They all drank from their cups in celebration, and Tarimev took the opportunity to examine his new pauldron. He inspected every inch of it, trying to commit this moment to his memory forever. When he was done, he got himself a mug of ale, took a seat to the side of the room and watched the dancing.

Once everyone had returned to the frivolities, Ebbina came and sat beside him. Her eyes were moist as she said, "You do not know how grateful I am. If not for you, we would be dead by now. I cannot express just how much your efforts mean to me, the tribe, and our future."

Tarimev looked to the floor, embarrassed by the attention, "It was nothing, Your Majesty. I merely reacted to the situation like any other soldier would."

"If you think that is what happened, you are wrong. Any other soldier of your people would have left me to die, glad to be rid of the Barbarian Queen. But you didn't, you saved me. The fact that you did it while outnumbered speaks volumes about your character. That is why I say; you are a hero."

Tarimev felt a lump in his throat, unable to speak.

Ebbina leaned towards him and gave him a kiss on the cheek, "Go, enjoy yourself. Dance with the women, they will love you."

He kissed her hand and said, "Thank you Your Majesty, but I shan't. You see, there is already a woman who draws my eye."

"I understand," Ebbina said, smiling wryly, "Might I see that thing you used against Eshami?"

He drew his pistol and handed it to her, "It's called a pistol, it uses black powder to fire a metal pellet at your enemies." Ebbina inspected the weapon, "It is an impressive weapon. I think I can trust you to keep it." She handed the weapon back, and her fingertips lingered as they brushed against Tarimev's. Ebbina smiled at him again and walked away, leaving Tarimev to re-join the celebrations.

Imre saw Tarimev approaching and bowed, "Well met, Yevan. Allow me to introduce myself. I am Marçhal Imre Rein, ambassador for the Marçhal Order."

Tarimev laughed at his friend's formal introduction, "Don't start with that, please. I'm very well aware of who you are."

Imre feigned a look of shock, "In that case, allow me to formally extend my gratitude for saving me, and for rescuing the Queen," he laughed and then dropped the fake expression. "Well done, friend. Who would have ever thought, two boys from Burtop would become high ranking members of the Yevanti Tribe?"

Tarimev smiled, "I can picture our classmates' faces now."

"Ah yes, the good old days."

Tarimev slapped Imre on the back, "Those were

indeed the good old days."

Imre looked to the Queen, then back to Tarimev, "You seem to be getting on well with Ebbina, if you catch my meaning."

Tarimev shrugged, "She is a lovely woman, but a gentleman doesn't speak of such matters."

Imre laughed, "So there are such matters. I will pry no more, you'll tell me yourself when you are drunk enough. Go, enjoy the feast."

He went off to find more of his friends, while Tarimev remained in the hall, drinking ale with his new tribesmen.

Torvald grew frustrated and drew his sword before pointing it at Daykon, "The King has no time for games."

Daykon pushed the Princess towards Torvald, "Take her then, but enjoy trying to leave. My guards will make sure you never get past them. You may as well surrender now."

Torvald used his unarmed hand to strike Daykon in the face, sending him falling backwards to the floor. As he fell, so too did his hat from his head, revealing his full face. His hook fell from his grip also, revealing his hand below. Captain Wilek also drew his sword and walked closer to Daykon.

He looked to Torvald and said, "I told you that something was off. That isn't the Pirate King. Isn't that right, Thierry?"

The man Torvald believed to be Daykon smirked, "So you do recognise me, Artemus."

Wilek nodded, "You must have been terrified when you saw me. Worried I'd expose you?"

"It's no matter, my men know who I am. They will fight to the death to protect me."

"That's good to hear, because I still have orders to kill you, as well as a personal interest in it, of course."

"And you believe that I could not stop you?"

"Perhaps you should look around, Artemus," said Torvald, "This is hardly the best time."

Wilek looked round, seeing dozens of pirates surrounding them, all armed with weapons. He turned back to Thierry, "I'm sorry, Torvald, but I need to kill him."

Thierry laughed, "Then you will die here, but if it makes you feel better-" He was interrupted by cannon fire, and shots striking the village. Torvald looked to see a ship rounding the coast had begun firing upon the village.

"What's going on? Who are they?" Torvald asked Wilek.

"Aylu," Wilek snarled through gritted teeth, "He's the lieutenant for the real pirate king. He must have heard about this impersonator. Go! Get the princess out of here."

Torvald didn't respond. He grabbed Cayte by the hand and helped her run into the streets nearby, moving through alleyways and hiding behind buildings as they tried to avoid the incoming cannons.

Soon the cannons ceased firing, and the fighting began. The crew of the Silver Eagle had landed on the shore and commenced their attack. Wilek broke away and fled in a different direction, while Torvald continued escorting the Princess. Torvald and the Princess neared the tree where he had left his horse and he untied the reins. He mounted it, before helping

Cayte mount it as well.

In one motion, Torvald turned the horse around and kicked it into a gallop, hoping to leave behind the chaos in Sosek.

As the night began to die down, and the Yevanti people returned to their homes, Tarimev remained in the Great Hall. He was sat comfortably in a chair, thinking he was alone, when Queen Ebbina sat down next to him.

She smiled, "Hello Yevan. I trust you had a good time."

Tarimev laughed, "Indeed. The food has been delicious, and the company entertaining."

Ebbina looked to him, "You seem very relaxed. Are you certain you aren't just drunk?"

Tarimev laughed, "Far from it. Perhaps I am drunk on your beauty, though."

"Then perhaps you shouldn't drink any more ale tonight."

"Why not? It seems to be working wonders for me."

Ebbina laughed, "I apologise for my lack of response earlier, you surprised me. I don't usually have men flirting so openly with me. Then again, I too often get so embroiled in my duties that no-one has ever had much chance."

"I couldn't resist, I am sorry."

"There is no need to apologise, you were merely being honest to your feelings," Ebbina leaned closer to him, her hand resting on his shoulder. She stared deeply into his eyes, and he could feel himself growing weak. Slowly, she kissed him, and he felt the kiss burning itself into his mind and soul. The kiss lasted several moments, until finally they pulled apart.

"I have to admit, that was pleasant," Ebbina said.

"It certainly was," replied Tarimev.

Ebbina smiled, "When do you leave Qoan?"

"Tomorrow morning, I must complete my quest soon. Though I shall miss your company."

Ebbina stepped close to him again, "Come and see me before you leave? The tribe will send you off properly."

Tarimev smiled, "Of course. I will be happy to oblige." She smiled back at him and the two of them sat until the early hours of the morning, talking about everything under the sun. By the time Tarimev left for bed, he felt he knew Ebbina better than he knew anyone else.

19

After breakfast, Tarimev dressed in his armour and made his way back to the Great Hall. He entered the room and walked up to Ebbina, who was seated on her throne. He bowed to her, "Your Highness."

"Good morning, Yevan," Ebbina remarked with a smile on her lips as she stood up from the table. She moved towards him and embraced him tightly, kissing his cheek affectionately. "I take it you had a good night?"

Tarimev nodded. "Yes, Your Highness, I did. Is this appropriate?"

Ebbina smiled again and released from the embrace. "Why shouldn't it be? We are not in Worthervir, we don't have protocols for such things here."

Tarimev grinned widely, then looked around the hall. "I will miss this place. I have only been here briefly, but I have enjoyed my time here."

"And why is that?" Ebbina asked curiously.

"Mostly the people," Tarimev replied sincerely.

Ebbina smiled as she turned and sat in her throne, motioning for him to move forward. "Yevan Tarimev, in order to complete your quest, you will be escorted to the Ashen Mountain by two of my best warriors; Marçhal Imre Rein, and my cousin, Prince Hodrin."

Marçhal Imre stepped forward from next to the throne, as did the tall warrior that Tarimev had seen the night before. On his back was a tarnished gold sword with a curved blade, and in his left hand was a small wooden shield, no more than two foot wide.

"Before you leave, you will need these," the Queen said as she produced Tarimev's sword and dagger from behind her throne.

Tarimev stared at the blade of his father's sword for a moment, then slowly accepted it. It had only been four days since he used it last, but it was heavier than he remembered, yet it still felt familiar. He held the weapon close and began to swing it experimentally, testing its weight and balance.

"I hope to see you again soon," the Queen said with a smile and a wink, "now you can continue your journey."

Tarimev nodded gratefully and turned back towards the door. "Thank you, Your Highness. I am grateful for all that you have done for me, and I will remember it for the rest of my days."

"You honour me with those words," Ebbina replied happily as she watched him leave.

Torvald and Cayte had ridden all night. Cayte had

fallen asleep on the back of the horse, but Torvald knew he couldn't sleep, despite his exhaustion, he had to get the Princess home. As the sun rose, Princess Cayte was roused from her sleep.

"Are we there yet?" She asked groggily.

"Halfway," Torvald replied, "we've just passed Calramon."

Cayte yawned and stretched, as if she'd been sleeping for days rather than hours. "That's good news, do you think it's safe to stop for a while? I'm starving!"

"I'm sorry, my love. I need to get you home first, but take a look in the saddlebag, there should be some bread in there."

The Princess reached into the bag hanging by her thigh. She found the loaf of bread and bit into it hungrily.

"How far is it now?" she asked, swallowing her mouthful.

"We'll be back in Alerill by nightfall," Torvald replied, "and it won't be too long after that until you're back in your bed in the palace. Now hold on, she's ready for a burst again I think."

Princess Cayte hugged tight onto Torvald's back and held on as he kicked his horse into a gallop.

Tarimev and his companions left Qoan immediately after leaving the Great Hall; the undergrowth of the Wilds was so thick that horses would not be able to pass through, so they travelled on foot. They trudged along the road towards the most dangerous parts of the Wilds, on their journey to the Ashen Mountain.

As the group walked through the forest, Tarimev was jolted from his thoughts by the sound of wild creatures snarling. All the men froze in fear and glanced nervously at each other, then heard the sounds of claws scraping against stone.

"What is that?" Tarimev whispered.

"There are wolves in the Wilds," Imre replied, "but they are unlikely to attack, they usually keep to themselves."

"It's not wolves, it sounds much bigger than that, and it's coming closer," Hodrin replied, "we need to hurry." He drew his sword and moved ahead quickly; ready to fight. The others followed suit.

They had barely moved ten paces when they saw the beast that had made the noise. It was twice the size of a wolf, and covered in black fur. Its head looked like that of a wolf, except its eyes were large and yellow. It stood up on its hind legs, almost as high as a man, to get a better view of them. The creature had two thick tusks protruding from its lower jaw.

The beast dropped back onto all-fours and charged at them, roaring menacingly. The three men tried to jump in different directions, to avoid the rushing creature but it was far faster than they were, and it knocked them all to the ground. Imre's sword fell from his hand as he hit floor. The beast stopped charging and turned to face them again, breathing heavily.

"Come on, move! We need to fight this, Lursans won't give up their prey," Hodrin yelled as he moved towards the beast.

The Lursan roared angrily, and Tarimev and Imre jumped to their feet. Imre picked up his sword; flames appeared along the blade and the red gem started to glow, illuminating the area around him and his eyes glowed the same colour as the gem. He stepped forward slowly, his sword held in front of him, ready to strike. "HODRIN! MOVE!" He shouted, with a voice full of authority. Hodrin ran to the side, away from the path of Imre.

The beast reared onto its hind legs, growling at the sight of the Marçhal, who was now advancing towards it. Imre raised his left hand, which had become engulfed by flame. He thrust his hand forward, and a ball of flame shot forth, striking the creature in the chest. It screamed and stumbled backwards, but continued to advance towards the Marçhal, who moved closer to it, his sword held defensively in front of him. The creature charged at Imre, but he dodged to the right, avoiding the blow. He swung his sword at the creature's head. The hot blade sliced through one of its tusks, making the Lursan roar in pain. It reared backwards to avoid another attack from Imre, while the other two men rushed towards it.

Hodrin and Tarimev attacked the creature together, swinging their swords at the beast, but it managed to dodge both blows. The beast stood upright, using its powerful forelimbs to strike at the men with its massive paws, knocking down both warriors. Tarimev rolled over, putting a small amount of distance between him and the beast, while Hodrin leapt to his feet, swinging his sword at it again. This time the blade cut deep into the creature's left flank, causing it to fall to the ground, bleeding profusely. The three men breathed a sigh of relief before the beast struggled to rise to its feet and turned to face Tarimev, ready to rip his throat out. It stepped slowly towards Tarimev, growling loudly, while Tarimev raised his sword in defence. The Lursan prepared to strike, but was again struck by a fireball from Marçhal Imre. The fire burned into its right eye, blinding it. Tarimev swung his sword at the beast's neck, cutting deep but not severing it. Imre ran towards the beast and plunged his blade into its chest, piercing its heart. The Lursan let out a loud yelp and collapsed to the ground.

The three men stared at the dead beast for a moment, before turning to look at each other.

"Are you alright?" Hodrin asked Tarimev.

Tarimev nodded.

Imre sheathed his sword, and as soon as his hand came off the hilt, the flames surrounding him receded. "I think we should keep moving."

Hodrin gathered some meat from the Lursan's body, then the three companions walked in silence through the forest, fortunately encountering no more difficulties until, finally, night fell and they couldn't see more than an arm's length ahead of themselves. "Hodrin, is there anywhere safe that we can spend the night?" asked Tarimev.

"I'm afraid I don't know. We are deeper into the forest than any Yevanti has been for generations."

"If we have to continue, then so be it. But maybe it's best if we rest here tonight, and start our journey in the morning." said Imre.

"Very well, let's make camp here," Hodrin replied. "We'll light a small fire, and cook what we have gathered," Tarimev stated.

They got to work making a fire and cooking some of the meat they had gotten from the Lursan. They ate in silence, the sounds of nature filling their ears. When finished, Tarimev removed his chestplate and lay down to sleep.

As dusk fell, Torvald and Cayte saw the walls of Alerill on the horizon. Cayte felt her spirits lift, knowing that soon she would be back home. She had never doubted that Torvald would save her; but her time with the false Pirate King was worse than anything she had faced before.

Torvald took one hand off the reins and placed it on Cayte's thigh reassuringly. "You will be home soon, my love."

Cayte smiled at his touch.

He returned back to focusing on the road ahead of them. The sun was setting, casting shadows across the land and making it difficult to see. Yet the silhouette of Alerill guided him along the road. As darkness descended upon him, he could just about make out the outline of the city walls.

He rode through the gates, straight through the city to the palace. He climbed off his horse and helped Cayte down. The guards looked surprised to see him, but he was quickly ushered into the dining hall, where the King awaited.

Occime was standing in front of the fireplace, holding a cup of wine in his hands. He turned around as Torvald entered, and ran to his daughter, embracing her as tears streamed down his face.

"Father," cried Cayte, burying her head in his chest. "I thought I'd never see you again!"

"I swear on all the gods, I would never let anything happen to you," Occime told her, before looking at Torvald, "Thank you for saving her, son."

Torvald nodded, unsure of how to respond.

"I apologise for my reaction the other day. If you

truly love my daughter, you have my full support. However, first I need you to go to the Halled Mountains and persuade the Dwarves to send ships to Alerill."

"Of course, Your Highness, but why do we need ships?"

"We won't be able to attack the Free Islands without the help of the dwarves. We need ships from Forlerin and the Halled Mountains to enact revenge."

"Your Highness, it wasn't the Pirate King who kidnapped Cayte, it was some criminal called Thierry. He was attacked by the lieutenant of the Pirate King, and I doubt he survived. An attack on the Free Islands would provoke an unnecessary war." Torvald said, before he went on to explain everything that happened on his journey. When he was done, the King sat down, rubbing the bridge of his nose.

"The Kingdom certainly would struggle in a war, our soldiers are spread out across the nation and our navy is full of merchants. What do you suggest we do?" he asked of Torvald.

"Nothing. The men responsible for this plot are defeated, and Cayte is safe. We should move on."

"I will trust you if you are certain this is the case. The two of you should go get some rest, I will speak to you tomorrow."

Torvald bowed to the King and followed Cayte out of the room towards his chambers, eager to finally sleep.

Tarimev had rested well, even on the cold floor of the Wilds, and awoke as the sun broke through the canopy above him. He sat up and stretched, then looked over at Hodrin. He was hunched over a fire, cooking some food as Imre still slumbered.

"Have you slept?" Tarimev asked.

"I don't need it. This is your quest; I will do what I can to ensure you succeed. Wake the Marçhal, I will finish cooking."

Tarimev stood and walked over to Imre, gently shaking him awake. The man groggily opened his eyes and looked up at Tarimev. "That magic really took it out of me, I haven't done that in a while."

"Eat then. You will need all your strength for the day that is to come."

The three men sat and had their fill of meat and water before Tarimev put his armour on and smothered the fire.

Hodrin led the way deeper south into the Wilds, the forest getting denser and the undergrowth thickening. After a few hours the trees started to get sparser, and the plant life nearby was dying off. The ground became rocky and cracked, the sky turned dark and cloudy, and the air fell still. They stepped out of the woods and saw in front of them a large mountain, towering above the clouds and made of black rock.

A small path cut through the rocks leading to a door at the base of the mountain. The door was a huge slab of stone with a crack running through it.

"There it is," Hodrin said, "The Ashen Mountain."

Imre crouched down and examined the cracks. "These contain traces of dark magic," he whispered. "They're fresh, meaning the magic has been practised recently. It seems your magician is still residing here."

"This is where we must go," Tarimev said. "Come on, let us begin."

"I'm sorry, Yevan, I can't continue with you into the mountain. This mountain is forbidden for the tribe to step foot on, I have led you this far but I must leave you now. I will return to Qoan and wish you the best for your quest and journey back."

"There is nothing to apologise for, Hodrin. You must stand by your customs, but my destiny lies within the Ashen Mountain. I will see you in Qoan, and please, reassure your cousin that we are here safely."

Hodrin smiled and hit his chest with his fist while bowing his head.

Tarimev and Imre watched him walk back into the trees, then turned back to the Ashen Mountain. He looked upon the cracked door, and felt his heart quicken. The men walked up the path towards the door. As they got closer, Tarimev could see symbols carved into the rock surrounding it, and deep into the centre a hand-shaped indentation.

Tarimev placed his hand against the door. A surge of heat ran through his body, and he felt a wave of energy flow from the rock beneath his feet. His hand began to glow red, the symbols and cracks around him began to glow brighter and brighter until there was a red flash, and Tarimev was thrown backwards onto the ground.

He struggled to move as pain shot through every fibre of his being. He rolled across the ground and managed to sit up; he saw Imre standing over him.

"It's a magic door, what made you think you could open it?" Imre asked with a tone of derision in his voice.

"I have no idea how these things work! Magic isn't my forte."

Imre helped him to his feet and they walked back towards the door. Imre placed his left hand on his sword, causing the gem embedded within to glow, his right hand becoming engulfed in flame again. He placed his flaming hand onto the door, and the symbols and cracks started glowing blue. As the light got stronger the door warped into the side of the mountain, like clay being shaped. When it was finished, there was a hole in the side of the rock big enough for them to pass through.

Torvald was used to sleeping rough when working away from the capital, but to not sleep at all for two days had taken its toll. When he awoke in his bed, he didn't want to get up, so he remained lying down.

As he lay, he could hear muffled voices talking outside his bedroom door. He was forced to get up when the door opened and King Occime walked inside. He leaped from his bed, wearing nothing but his cloth trousers, and bowed as the King stood at the foot of the bed looking down at him.

"Please get up, Sir Storheam."

Torvald quickly pulled on an undershirt. "I'm sorry, Your Majesty, I did not realise you would be here this morning. What brings you here?"

Occime smiled and walked over to Torvald, placing his hands on either side of his face. "You look well rested, my good knight. How did you fare last night? I hope it was enough?"

Torvald looked confused. "Why, yes, thank you Your Majesty. I slept very well."

Occime removed his hands from Torvald and walked over to look out the window. "Good, I am glad to hear that. I have been thinking about your quest to rescue my daughter, and how you handled it. I don't believe that any other soldier would have travelled as swiftly as you did to reach her. I would like to tell you, if you are willing, that I would like for you to join my family." He turned to face Torvald, awaiting a response.

Torvald sat on the edge of his bed, smiling. "Your Majesty, I accept the offer with great pleasure. I would like nothing more, I love Cayte with all of my heart and I couldn't imagine a life without her."

"Excellent. It is settled then. I will leave you to ask Cayte to marry you, and I hope she accepts."

"Thank you, Your Majesty, I will do as you say."

Occime smiled and placed his hands on Torvald's shoulders. "You are a fine man, Torvald. Do not forget that."

Occime left the room and closed the door behind him. Torvald went over to his wardrobe and picked out the best clothes he could find. He put them on, then knocked on Cayte's door next to his own. She came to the door and opened it.

"Torvald, what are you doing here so early?" Her eyes were wide with surprise.

Torvald smiled, "Cayte, I have an important question to ask you."

She nodded slowly and walked back into her room. Torvald followed her into the room and closed the door.

"I have spoken to your father this morning, regarding our relationship. I would like to know if you will become my wife."

Cayte looked at him with an expression of shock

and disbelief before kissing him passionately on the lips. "Yes," she whispered. "Yes, of course I'll marry you."

They embraced each other again, and laughed together.

"Thank you," said Torvald, "I love you."

"And I love you." They kissed again before Torvald took a step back. "We should tell your father about your answer. I presume there is a lot to plan?"

"There certainly is. We need to arrange a suitable day, and then the lords of the world should be told. It may take some time, but we have plenty of time to prepare."

"We can tell your parents at breakfast; I'll see you down there."

Torvald kissed her again and left the room, walking back to his own quarters. He thought about his future with Cayte and smiled to himself.

20

The inside hall of the Ashen Mountain was surprisingly well-lit, albeit by a green glow that seemed to come from nowhere. Tarimev and Imre made their way through the empty cavern to a small opening in the wall with a torch above it. At this point, the two men stopped and looked at each other for several seconds. Both were very nervous; one out of fear, the other out of curiosity. Finally, Tarimev took the torch from above the opening and stepped through. He held the torch high as he moved forward into blackness, and Imre followed behind him. Once in the corridor, they could hear whispering around them but could see nothing. For a while, the two men proceeded cautiously down the long corridor until they reached stone stairs leading upwards. They slowly ascended the stairs, afraid of what awaited above.

When they finally arrived at the top of the steps,

there was another pause before either man would venture forth to take the first step. This time it was Imre who entered first, and as soon as he entered the room he was enveloped in fog. Tarimev rushed in to aid his friend but was also surrounded by fog. When the thick grey mist moved away to the edges of the room, Tarimev found himself alone, in a circular chamber. The floor was covered in carved stone blocks that glowed softly in the dark. There were three openings in the wall that each led to a dark void. Each opening had a number above it that was glowing green.

Tarimev walked through the first opening and it led him back to the streets of Burtop at dusk, looking just as he remembered. His clothing felt lighter, and he looked down to see that he was wearing his old farming clothes. He turned around to return to the mountain, only to see that the opening he had come through was no longer there. It was then, that he heard music coming from the direction of the town square. He walked the quiet streets for a while, trying to find the source of the melody. The further into the village he travelled, the more that the mountain felt like a fading dream. Soon enough he arrived in the Town Square to see a village festival in full swing, and he stood and watched the dancers. The music was beautiful. A band of musicians sat on the edge of the stage playing instruments that resembled a wind instrument, and as he looked around the square, he noticed many people sitting and enjoying themselves. He heard the shout of glee from a child and turned to see a young girl running towards him. She threw herself onto Tarimev, laughing as she hugged him tightly.

"Daddy!" the little girl cried happily. "You're here!"

Tarimev looked at the girl in confusion. He opened his mouth to ask her who she was, when he heard a familiar voice say, "Darling, where've you been?"

He looked up and saw his childhood love, Melane, walking towards him with a baby in her arms. Her brown hair had grown down to her chest since he last saw her, and her face was radiant with happiness. She smiled warmly and said, "I'm so glad you made it." She kissed him on the cheek and gave the toddler a tight hug.

Tarimev thought back to his childhood; the last time he had seen Melane they were both sixteen years old. She was leaving Burtop and her family to move to the Cascuran Kingdom, to study at the Royal Academy. He had always regretted not telling her how he felt about her.

Melane took him by the hand and led him to a bench in the middle of the square where they sat down. The little girl climbed onto the bench between them and began talking about all sorts of things.

Tarimev couldn't help but smile as the girl recounted her day to him, and he listened intently to all of the details she told him. It was a wonderful feeling, to have someone to talk to, who cared for him like Melane seemed to, yet he still couldn't help but feel that something was wrong. The little girl drifted off to sleep in Melane's lap after a long while.

As if reading his mind, Melane said, "You see what you missed out on?"

Tarimev shook his head in confusion, "What do you mean?"

Melane reached over and gently stroked his cheek. "This is what you could have had if you had been brave enough to tell me how you felt."

Tarimev looked at Melane with sadness in his eyes. She looked back at him, and her features began to melt away. The world around him became distorted and blurred. He stood from the bench in terror, falling backwards as he went unconscious.

Imre found himself in a room similar to that which Tarimev had been in, though he didn't know it. Ahead of him were two openings into a dark void. He hesitated for a moment before choosing the left one, and stepped through.

He found himself standing on a large balcony overlooking the Garden City of Askerskali, no longer wearing the robes and armour of a Marçhal but plain, grey, mage's robes. Below him was a city made up of white marble buildings and wide roads. The walls of almost every building were covered in green plants, and there were flowers everywhere. The air was filled with sweet scents that seemed to lift his spirits. Looking down from his perch on the balcony, he saw hundreds of people going about their business. As he looked around, he realised that he must be standing in the mage's tower of the Askerskali Palace.

Imre left the balcony and walked into the room behind him. It was large and circular, fifteen feet high with walls lined in bookshelves. The room was filled with ancient looking scrolls and tomes. In the centre of the room was a table, upon which rested a book and a glass orb. Imre walked over and picked up the book. It was bound in leather, and the title was written in gold letters; 'The Book of Mages'. He picked up the book to read it when the door opened. An old man with a long white beard walked in. He wore a cloak and ornate robes that were emerald green with yellow trim. His head was covered by a cowl, and he carried a staff with a blue crystal mounted on the top. He looked very much like a wizard. His blue eyes sparkled as he looked at Imre.

"Good to see you this morning, apprentice," he said in a low voice.

Imre looked at him incredulously. "Who are you? Where am I?"

The old man laughed at him. "A little too much to drink at the feast last night? Come, we have much to do today."

The old man gestured for Imre to follow him, and began to leave. Imre stayed where he was, confused and unsure of what was happening. The old man turned back and said, "Something seems wrong with you, boy. Are you feeling okay?"

"Of course not. This isn't right."

The old man sighed and said, "Would you care to elaborate?"

"This isn't real, I have never been here before. I was in the Ashen Mountain, and now I'm here."

The old man frowned, "Interesting. Continue."

Imre explained everything to the wizard. When he was finished, the old man nodded his head and said, "That's interesting. It seems as though you are trapped in a dreamscape. You really have no idea who I am? Or how we know each other?"

"No, I don't."

The old man looked at him strangely. "My name is

Abano, I am the Court Mage for the Republic of Amargond. I took you in as my apprentice when you were caught trying to steal from the Royal Treasury. You were offered a place in the Marçhal order when the Marçhal who caught you sensed your abilities. But you refused, and instead of sending you to jail I took you in. I am training you to become an expert in all areas of magic, not just a handful like the Marçhals would teach you."

"I went with that Marçhal, and I joined the order. But I did always wonder what would have happened if I hadn't joined that day."

Abano smiled and said "Have you ever regretted your decision?"

Imre thought for a few moments and said, "A few times over the years."

"That must be it then. This dark wizard you are hunting has laid traps; I think you are in a world created by your regrets. You said there were two doors, and I believe each one must represent a regret. If you want to leave here, and the next illusion, find what is different between the world created and your world. Focus on the positives of what came of your decision."

Imre closed his eyes. He thought of his reunion with Tarimev, his times with the Yevanti and all the times he helped people as a Marçhal. He thought of his friends within the Marçhal Order, and how proud his parents were when he became a Marçhal Ambassador. He felt wind rushing around him and the sounds of the city faded away. He opened his eyes to find himself back in the mountain, in front of the two openings.

Tarimev opened his eyes and was laying on the floor, in front of the three openings. With no other way to go, he stood to his feet and walked through the second door. In the blink of an eye, he was standing in a large garden, decorated with flowers and plants he had never seen before. Again, his armour had vanished yet this time he was wearing clothes befitting of a noble. At the centre of the garden was a large fountain surrounded by rocks and some flowers blooming along its edge. There were tall trees at the far end of the garden, which provided good shade from the sun. The garden was well maintained by the gardeners that were trimming the bushes, and it looked like it belonged to a rich man or woman. Behind him was a palatial building, framed with wood and stone. As Tarimev stared in awe at this building, a man came out of the house and bowed to him.

"My Lord," the man said, smiling, "You have a visitor in your study."

Tarimev followed the man inside the building. He was led through corridors lined with paintings and sculptures. The man, who Tarimev had realised by now was a servant, stopped and opened a door before ushering him inside. Tarimev stepped into the room and saw it was a large study, with a gold-trimmed wooden desk covered in papers, and a matching chair behind it. Sitting with his back to the door was a man with greying hair and expensive-looking clothes. Tarimev wasn't sure what to do, but a feeling at the back of his mind made him want to sit at the desk. He walked over to the chair and sat down.

The servant placed his hand on the doorknob, and

asked "Would you like some wine, my lord? Perhaps some from the elven collection."

Tarimev nodded at the servant who bowed and left the room. He looked at the man seated opposite him, an elderly man, and saw someone who looked remarkably similar to Torvald.

"Thank you for seeing me," said the man, "I assume you know why I am here."

"I don't even know why I'm here."

"Well, allow me to introduce myself. I am Lord Elmont Storheam, and before you sold your farm and started your company, I was the largest merchant in Worthervir. I have come to propose that we merge our companies together into one, allowing us to offer a wider selection of goods and services to a larger customer base. It will also mean that I can use your expertise to expand my business further, allowing me to grow even more rapidly than I already am."

Tarimev smiled at him and said, "I'm sorry, I really don't know what's going on."

Lord Elmont waved his hand dismissively and said, "I understand that you are a busy man, so I shall get straight to the point. I would offer you three thousand Linya to buy into your company, and allow you to expand it further."

Tarimev didn't know what to say, he had no idea what was going on, but he couldn't believe that he was being offered so much money without having to lift a finger. With that sort of money, he could buy the land under Burtop, and all the property on it. He had never seen any amount of money like that before, and likely never would again. As these thoughts passed through his mind, another servant entered the office with a tray holding a silver jug and two silver goblets.

"Your wine, sir."

The servant poured the wine and handed one of the goblets to Tarimev and the other to Lord Elmont. Lord Elmont took a sip of his own wine and said, "Now you know why I am here. Tell me, do you see what you could have had? If only you had decided to sell your farm, look at the riches you could have obtained. How wonderful your life would have been."

Elmont smiled nefariously as Tarimev, once again, looked on in horror as the man in front of him seemed to melt away and his vision blurred, before fading entirely.

Imre didn't hesitate before he walked through the second opening in front of him. He didn't know what to expect, but he knew how to get out. As he stepped through, he was in what looked like military barracks. The floor was tiled in flagstone, and the walls were covered in wooden boards. The room was lit with torches stuck into brackets next to each of the beds. Imre looked down to check his clothes and saw that he was wearing armour similar to that of Tarimev's. He had a sword on his left hip and a shield on his back. Across the room, Imre could see a set of double doors. He walked over to them and pushed on them. They swung open, into the lively streets of an unknown city. He could hear the clatter of carts and the shouts and cries of people selling their wares.

Imre looked around, and as he did so three soldiers ran out from behind a building, heading somewhere with purpose. "Recruit, follow us!" yelled one of the men as another grabbed his shoulder and pulled him with them. He did as he was told and ran with the soldiers until they emerged from the streets in a market square where a mass brawl had broken out between a group of merchants and a street gang.

"Bring them down!" shouted the soldier next to Imre, and the others rushed to obey. They had swords drawn and charged into the gang members. The street thugs prepared as the soldiers advanced. One of the gang members tried to run, but the nearest soldier tackled him and punched him in the face, knocking him out cold. Imre was watching the chaos unfold when he felt something strike the back of his head. He fell forwards to the ground, and felt someone raining blows down on the back of his head. He was trying not to pass out when the attack on him stopped. He rolled onto his back and looked up to see the fight was over, and the man who had attacked him was lying on his back, being beaten by Tarimev. Imre struggled to his feet and called out to his friend.

"Tarimev, you're here."

Tarimev looked at him. "What happened? How did he get the jump on you?"

"He hit me from behind, I'm so pleased to see you. Now we can get out of here and find the dark wizard."

Tarimev looked at Imre with a concerned expression. "Are you alright? What are you talking about?"

"We need to leave this place; it isn't safe for us here."

"We can't leave Alerill yet, we need to finish our training."

Imre looked around him. "No, Tarimev, this place isn't real. We have to get back to the mountain."

"Come on, let's get you a drink." Tarimev put his arm around Imre and escorted him to a tavern across the square, much to Imre's protestations.

The two friends sat opposite each other at a table in the corner of the tavern, sipping from a glass of ale. Tarimev watched Imre closely and said, "You seem different somehow, Imre. Are you sure you're alright?"

"Please listen to me," replied Imre, "We are not really here. We are in the Ashen Mountain on the way to defeat a necromancer."

Tarimev looked confused. "I don't understand. How can that be?"

"Just trust me. This place is a dream we've both been having. You must be dreaming now too. Think, surely you realise that this doesn't match up with your memory."

"I don't know what you are talking about, this life matches perfectly with my memory."

Imre's eyes widened as a realisation came to him, "Of course, you're part of the dream. It makes perfect sense, after all, we wouldn't share a regret with each other. We haven't seen each other for almost ten years."

"You can't be serious, Imre. We've been friends since childhood, aside from when you lived in Askerskali."

Imre shook his head. "No, we haven't. Alright, tell me about my life since I left Burtop."

"We should get you to a healer, I think that fight caused some damage."

Imre sighed with frustration. "Tarimev, friend, please humour me."

"Alright, where do you want me to start?"

"When I left Burtop, I was fifteen, yes?"

Tarimev nodded, "Yes, you moved to Askerskali with your family at fifteen, but you came back to Burtop on your own at sixteen, something to do with pressure from a gang. You moved in with me and my father, and you helped us on the farm. You stayed with me once my father died. Then when Burtop was attacked, and the farm destroyed, we came to Alerill together to become knights. Are you happy now? Will you drop your delusion?"

Imre said nothing, but closed his eyes and focused on what was missing from this life. He thought of his magic, but most of all he thought of his wife. As he remembered his wedding day, he felt the same wind as in the last dream.

For the second time, Tarimev was on the floor in front of the openings to the void. There was only one opening he hadn't tried; he knew it would likely lead to another strange timeline but he had no other way to go. He stepped through, prepared to not understand the world he was in, and in front of him were the doors to the throne room of Worthervir. He was wearing the same armour he was wearing back in the mountain and still had his sword at his side. He pushed the doors open and inside the throne room were hundreds of people, and they immediately erupted into applause and cheers when they saw Tarimev in the doorway. At the far end of the room, the King stood in front of his throne and he motioned for Tarimev to approach. Tarimev walked through an aisle in between the crowd and stopped in front of King Occime.

"Tarimev, how good to see you again. Congratulations on the arrest of Shrave, we have been trying to find him for many years. In honour of you defeating such a high-profile criminal, it has been decided that you will become a Knight of Alerill, and you will not have to partake in a trial."

Tarimev bowed. "Thank you, Your Majesty."

The King stood and walked towards Tarimev. "Do you see what could have been? If you hadn't killed him, if you had simply arrested him, you would be a hero by now. You wouldn't be risking your life for redemption."

Tarimev looked at the King, knowing what was about to happen, and as expected the King's features melted away and Tarimev felt himself slipping into unconsciousness.

When he awoke this time, the openings had disappeared and Imre stood beside him. He got to his feet as fast as he could and was about to speak when an ethereal voice said, "You have seen how your lives could have been. Tell me which was your greatest regret and you can stay in that world for the rest of your life."

"None of them," said Tarimev.

Imre gave a small smile and said, "I agree. I don't regret anything anymore."

"If everything that happened to me hadn't happened, I wouldn't be here now. There were bad moments but there were also good times, and I will never give those up," Tarimev continued, resolute in his belief.

There was a large gust of wind and the fog around the room dissipated, revealing another set of stairs in

The Trials of Knights

front of the two men.

Torvald made his way downstairs and entered the dining hall, where the Princess was already eating with her parents. He bowed his head to the King and Queen as Cayte gave him a welcoming smile from across the room. He took his seat next to her and she nodded toward her parents. Torvald could tell she wanted him to break the news, she seemed nervous but he knew they would be pleased. He looked over at them and saw the King and Queen smiling happily at him.

He stood up and walked over to the King and Queen. "Your Majesties, we have something to tell you both. Princess Cayte and I have decided to get married."

The King and Queen's faces soon lit up with smiles. The King said, "That's wonderful! Congratulations!"

Queen Lorea was crying tears of joy. "I am so happy for you both. We have lots of work to get started on, a royal wedding is no small affair."

"I will make the announcement to the people this afternoon. We have our monthly ball tonight where we were going to celebrate the return of Cayte," said the King. "But we shall treat it as a celebration of your engagement as well."

"I am sure the guests will enjoy that," added the Queen, as she neatly placed her knife and fork on her plate, "Come, my dear, let's see if we can get started on some arrangements." Lorea and Cayte stood from the table and made their way out of the dining hall.

Torvald remained seated and watched them go, before turning to the King. "Is there any news of

Tarimev? Cayte told me that he had been given a dangerous task. Has he returned yet?"

King Occime shook his head. "Sorry, Torvald, we haven't heard anything yet. Mr Riswaell is a fine warrior; I am sure he will return in time."

"Where has he gone?" Torvald asked.

"I'm not at liberty to say, not until he returns. I can tell you that he is doing the kingdom a great service. Now go, you have much to plan."

"Of course, Your Majesty."

Torvald stood up and bowed to the King before making his way out of the palace. He knew that he should be happy about being engaged to such a beautiful woman, but all he could think about was Tarimev's absence. Was he in trouble? Or worse, dead?

21

After climbing for what felt like a week, Tarimev and Imre reached the top of the stairs to find a vast hall with a high ceiling. The huge room was again lit by a green glow coming from nowhere in particular. It did not illuminate the chamber, but rather seemed to permeate everything around them. Another set of stairs was on the far side of the hall, leading up into darkness. In the centre of the hall was a pedestal, above which floated a black gem with a faint white glow surrounding it.

"I didn't expect there to be this much inside the mountain. This necromancer has protected himself well." Tarimev said, his voice echoing off the vaulted roof.

Imre agreed, "Yes, we should be prepared for anything here." He scanned the walls and ceiling as he spoke. There were no obvious weapons or traps anywhere in sight, but he knew better than to underestimate a necromancer's capabilities. They had both seen how powerful the dark magic could be when used against them.

The two of them began to walk towards the stairs at the far end of the chamber. And as they walked, the light from the gem in the middle of the hall grew stronger and brighter. The two men stopped and stared as they observed their surroundings. An orb of light shot from the gem, like an ember from a fire, and landed a few feet away from them. The orb slowly got brighter and began to form the shape of a human figure. Four more orbs of light shot out of the gem and started to form human shapes. Tarimev and Imre watched as the ghostly figures' faces morphed into having detailed features. Their faces looked familiar, though they couldn't quite place who they were.

"What is going on?" Tarimev asked.

The ghostly figures continued to take the shape of people until eventually, all five were recognisable as people they knew. All five figures were standing in a line in front of the two men who, unsure of what was happening, had both drawn their swords.

They looked at the figures in front of them when Tarimev pointed to the one in the middle, shocked, "That's Ebbina." He looked at the other two standing next to her, "and they are people I know too; that's Torvald, and..." He trailed off as he looked at the figure on the end.

Imre eyes widened. "Is that Cosai?"

"It is. It's my father," Tarimev said trying to hold back tears.

"I know these two as well," Imre said, looking at

the figures in front of him. "That's Grandmaster Bromel, and that's my wife."

All of the figures stood still, staring at the two men, who were now both confused.

"What do you want? Why are you here?" Tarimev asked.

The ghostly figures made no response and continued standing in front of the two men.

"Why don't you say something?" Tarimev asked them, his voice barely above a whisper.

Still nothing.

Torvald sat with Cayte in the royal study, discussing potential ideas for the wedding. He was thoroughly bored and was starting to worry about what would become of his career once he was married. After all, he wouldn't be able to continue serving as a knight once he was the husband of the future queen of the kingdom.

But Cayte wasn't sharing his concerns. She had been excited since he proposed that morning, and had been happily discussing possibilities for their future together ever since. The only thing she was concerned about was the fact that they hadn't yet set a date.

"When do you think we should have our wedding?" Cayte asked excitedly.

"We could ask the King if he wants to marry us tomorrow," Torvald joked, "we could skip all this planning then."

She laughed, "That might be fun, but I'm enjoying the planning. The wait will be worth it."

"How long do you think it'll take to get everything ready?"

"I don't know, maybe six months?"

"Six months?!" he exclaimed. "That seems like forever!"

"Don't worry, Father will put together a team of ministers to help plan the event. We can trust him to make sure everything runs smoothly."

"I hope so," he replied, "I am not really good at this sort of thing."

Cayte smiled at him, "You're doing great." She gave him a kiss on the cheek, "Leave me to this if you want, have some fun for once."

He thought about that for a moment before agreeing, "Ok. I'll go see what's happening in the city. Maybe there's a fight on in the docks."

After leaving the room, Torvald headed down the hallway and entered the throne room. He looked around and spotted his father stood before the throne. He hadn't seen him since he began his training as a knight, and he was glad of it. He was never close to his father due to his treatment of him as a child.

"Father," Torvald said in shock.

Lord Elmont turned and smiled at him, "Hello, son. His Majesty just told me your news."

"What are you doing here?"

"I'm here for the King's ball. I've not attended for years due to my company, but I'm nearing retirement now so I am stepping back." Lord Elmont replied.

"It is good to see you again, but I have to go, lots of planning to do."

"Of course, don't let me get in your way."

"No, it's fine."

As Torvald walked away, he couldn't help but smile. He never knew family life when he was younger, he only really saw his parents on official events, but when he thought about it, King Occime and Queen Lorea had accepted him into their family and treated him as a son. He continued towards the door to the city when he heard the King calling him.

"Sir Storheam! A moment please."

Torvald turned around and walked back to the king, "Yes Your Majesty?"

"I know my daughter is like her mother, I presume she has sent you away so she can continue planning on her own?"

"Yes, Your Majesty, that's correct."

"Please, less of the formalities when it is only us speaking. You are almost family, call me Occime when we are in private. If you are free, I would appreciate it if you would join me for a drink in my private chambers."

"Of course, Occime." Torvald said with a smile before following the King to his chambers.

The ghostly figures continued to stand perfectly still in front of the two men, making no sound.

"We should get to those stairs and get to the dark wizard," Tarimev whispered to Imre.

"I agree, but what about them?" Imre responded, gesturing to the figures in front of them with his sword.

"They seem harmless, they must be here only to scare us," Tarimev said, as he took a step towards the door. Once he did this, the ghostly figures all looked at him and weapons appeared in their hands. The apparition of Ebbina had a sword in either hand, while the rest of them all just had the one.

Tarimev raised his sword high, preparing to defend himself against the apparitions, when Cosai swung forward with his sword, directly towards Tarimev.

Cosai's strike was high, aiming right at Tarimev's head, but Tarimev's sword was already up and ready to block the attack. The force of Cosai's swing was too much, and the edge of the sword struck his blade, knocking him down to his knees.

Imre was quick to react, charging forward to assist his friend, when all the other apparitions attacked. Bromel and Jarea were the closest to him so both moved together to flank him. He blocked a blow from one of them before swinging his sword out sideways to hit the side of another figure. It was hard to tell which of them it was, but he felt his sword connect with something surprisingly solid. Tarimev got back to his feet and went to thrust his sword at Cosai, but found himself unable to attack the apparition of his father. Instead, he backed away, uncertain how to proceed. The apparition of Torvald stepped forwards with his sword pointed at Tarimev's chest.

Imre was busy fighting the apparitions of both Bromel and Jarea, but he also couldn't bring himself to fight them so he merely dodged and blocked their strikes. He didn't have time to think about why they were attacking him, he was simply trying to stay alive.

Jarea swung her sword at Imre's head, but Tarimev managed to turn and block the strike for him. With one swift movement, Tarimev used his sword to push Jarea's blade above her head then pulled his sword back and slashed her from shoulder to hip. There was a burst of light, and Jarea's apparition disappeared in front of them. Imre felt a rush of grief, before his mind registered that it wasn't actually his wife that was just killed. He quickly turned to face Bromel when another orb of light shot out of the gem in the centre of the room and, slowly, Jarea's ghostly figure began to reform.

"We have to get the gem!" Imre shouted to Tarimev, who was currently defending himself from attacks from both Cosai and Torvald.

Imre tried to make a break for the gem but Ebbina slashed one of her swords upwards towards him, causing him to track back. Imre flicked his wrist to bring his sword down and deflect the attack. However, the force of the blow negated his block and pushed his sword arm up, with Ebbina's blade catching the underside of his forearm and slicing through his flesh, sending blood spurting across the floor.

Tarimev used his sword to deflect blow after blow from Cosai and Torvald when he saw Ebbina wound Imre. He whispered to himself, "I'm sorry, Dad," before stabbing forward with his sword and plunging it through the apparition of Cosai. The apparition burst into an explosion of light, and the gem immediately shot out an orb. Now faced with only Torvald, Tarimev drew his pistol from behind his back, before blocking an incoming attack from Torvald and kicking him backwards. He regained his balance, planted his feet, raised his pistol towards the gem, and fired.

The King's chambers, consisted of at least six rooms that could be seen just from the doorway. Torvald followed Occime through to a square room which simply had some comfortable-looking wingback chairs and a long table with many different bottles and crystal glasses on top. There was a window at the far end of the room which had a view out to the sea, and two chairs looking out the window with a small table in between them. Occime picked up a bottle of clear liquid and poured two glasses, before handing one to Torvald.

"Come, join me," Occime said with a smile as he sat in one of the chairs looking out the window.

Torvald smiled and took a seat. He clinked his glass against the King's, before taking a sip.

The liquid burned in his throat and almost made Torvald feel sick as he swallowed it down.

"What is this?" Torvald asked as he coughed from the taste of the drink.

"It's spirit wine. All the rage in Amargond I'm told," Occime said as he laughed at Torvald's reaction to the drink.

"Very popular amongst the nobility," he continued. "They say it's the best alcohol you can buy."

"I think I'd rather have a good ale," Torvald replied with a laugh, before gulping down more of the spirit wine.

Torvald and Occime sat quietly, their drinks in their hands as they looked out at the beautiful sea. Eventually, Occime looked over at Torvald.

"Be honest with me, how do you feel about the wedding?" Occime asked.

Torvald hesitated for a moment. "I love your daughter, with all my heart. I can't wait to spend the rest of my life with her. But I worry about what will become of my career, being a knight is all I ever wanted. Will I have to give it up?"

"You won't have to," Occime said confidently, "as

Prince of Worthervir you will be able to do whatever you would like. If you wish to continue serving as a knight, that is your choice. You will still have to attend official functions though."

"Thank you, that is good to hear."

Occime smiled and poured another drink for the two of them. They sat and chatted about nothing in particular for a while longer, until Occime stood from his chair.

"I should go and see how the preparations for the ball are coming along, but meet me in the war room shortly. There is something I would like your advice on. Welcome to the family, son," Occime smiled and shook Torvald's hand.

Tarimev's shot hit its mark and the gem shattered into pieces. The ghostly figures looked at the pedestal, before turning back to their opponents and attacking with more ferocity than before, while Ebbina continued to stand in front of the pedestal watching the fight. The apparition of Cosai had finished reforming, and re-joined the attack. Tarimev blocked the attacks of both Cosai and Torvald, but was forced backwards by their attacks. He backed up until he was near Imre and the two stood back-to-back, protecting themselves from the onslaught of blows from the apparitions.

Cosai swung his sword at Torvald's head, but Tarimev raised his blade to defend against the blow. He then stepped forward and kicked Cosai in the stomach, sending him flying back. Bromel sliced across at Imre, who brought his sword across his body to parry the attack.

The apparitions were relentless in their attacks, and Tarimev knew they wouldn't last much longer if they didn't defeat them. "We need to switch, I can't bring myself to kill them."

Imre agreed and the two men circled around to face the enemies of each other. Now facing Bromel and Jarea, Tarimev prepared to strike, unrestricted by emotion like before. He struck at Bromel first, forcing him backwards with a flurry of quick jabs. Then he turned to Jarea and attacked with more force, swinging his sword at her torso. She blocked the attack with her own blade and Bromel thrust his sword forward at Tarimev's chest. He stepped to the side and Bromel's attack sliced into his left shoulder.

Tarimev spun around and lunged at Bromel, slashing at his neck in a futile attempt to slice it open. Realising his mistake, he thrust forwards and plunged his sword through Bromel's chest. There was a burst of light, and the ghostly figure of Bromel disappeared.

Jarea's sword swept across at Tarimev's torso, glancing off his armour without causing any damage. She stepped back to make room for another attack, and Tarimev saw his opening. He swung his sword upwards at Jarea's face.

But she moved too fast for him, and knocked his sword away. He attacked again immediately, bringing the point of his sword down into her shoulder. She recoiled from the impact, but her movements were sluggish and slow. Tarimev jumped on top of her and drove his sword into her stomach, pushing her back onto the ground. The sword sunk halfway into her body, before she exploded into light and his sword struck the stone floor.

Meanwhile, Imre was defending himself from attacks from both Cosai and Torvald. He was no longer back-to-back with Tarimev, but still remained close enough to cover his friend. As the apparitions attacked, Imre looked for an opening in their defences.

He saw it when Torvald swung at his head, and he blocked it with his sword. He tried to push Torvald backwards, but his arms were too weak from his injury, and he couldn't overcome the apparition's strength. Imre turned his attention to Cosai instead. He watched as Cosai readied himself for another swing, and used the brief opening to stab his sword into the apparition's stomach. A second later, there was a flash of light and the apparition vanished.

Imre grinned triumphantly, but immediately felt a sharp pain shoot through his wounded arm. He had no time to tend to the wound, as Torvald's sword was arcing through the air towards him. He dropped to his knees and rolled under the blade, ending up behind Torvald. He stood up and stabbed his blade behind him, running it clean into Torvald's back. There was another burst of light and Torvald was gone.

Tarimev and Imre both turned their attention to Ebbina, who was now walking towards them with both swords at the ready.

Torvald arrived in the war room to see King Occime seated with High General Barra and Admiral Larstope. All three men were staring intently at a map of the eastern continent. Occime looked up at him, "Thank you for coming, Torvald. As you will soon be Prince of Worthervir, I have decided to bring you into the inner circle of my council."

"I am humbled to be included amongst such great men," said Torvald.

Barra spoke, "We've been investigating the rumours of ships sighted in the Veiled Ocean. We believe the reports are true, and from further reports it seems that the ships originate within the ocean itself. It seems there must be a society within the ocean that is yet to be made contact with."

Torvald nodded thoughtfully. He recalled stories of the Veiled Sea from what little he knew of his father's mercantile business. The sea was impassable due to a thick smog that made visibility poor, and it was impossible to navigate. The only known landmass within the sea was the Black Crater, a defunct volcano that erupted millennia ago, causing the ocean to become full of smoke, held there by ancient magic. If there were people living within the ocean, then surely, they would have developed some kind of technology that would allow them travel the sea. He wondered if perhaps the kingdom could use this knowledge to its advantage, and be able to navigate the whole world.

Larstope stood up, "That is not all. I have received word recently that some of the ships have been seen in the Gliss Tribelands and even near the Yevanti Wilds. These are areas we have never ventured into before, but if these people are enemies, then perhaps, we should consider making contact with the tribes in these areas. Perhaps they can give us information about how to deal with this threat."

Occime cleared his throat, "Are we sure that these people are threats? After all they have not attacked any of our cities or towns, nor do they seem to be spreading out beyond the ocean. They may just be traders seeking a safe haven to trade goods."

Barra nodded slowly, "I agree. Until we know more about them and what they want, we shouldn't go rushing into war with them."

Torvald rubbed his chin thoughtfully, "Perhaps we should wait and see if there is an increase in ships before we declare them enemies?"

The king nodded, "There is wisdom in your words, Torvald. I think we should keep in contact with the other nations and make sure we all stay informed of the situation. Is everyone agreed?"

All three men nodded, and the King continued, "Then that is what we shall do. Barra, I entrust you with the task of keeping in contact with the other nations. You are all dismissed." With those final words, Occime left the room.

Ebbina was ready to attack when Tarimev and Imre charged her, Tarimev on her left and Imre on her right. But she blocked all of their strikes and retaliated by pushing them away. She then launched herself at them, slicing across at Imre who blocked the blade, parrying the strike just in time. Tarimev's shoulder wound suddenly stung, he looked down to see blood running from his wound, and he winced in pain. He looked up to see Ebbina's blade about to strike his head, and leaped back to avoid it. But he was too late in his reaction, and the tip of her blade slashed across his left eye. He stumbled backwards, clutching his face, as blood dripped in front of his eye.

His vision impaired, he lunged forward desperately, slashing at his opponent. Ebbina spun around and brought a sword up to block the blow, but the force of the hit sent her reeling backwards. She recovered quickly, and proceeded to swing her sword in a low arc towards Tarimev's gut, but Imre defended his friend and blocked the cut. This gave Tarimev the opportunity to slash at Ebbina, who stepped back and thrust her sword upwards, pushing the strike away from her.

Imre screamed in rage, charging at her with a shout of vengeance, but she did not retreat and the two met with a flurry of blows, parries and blocks. Imre blocked her one sword with his own, but Ebbina stabbed at him with her other blade. Unable to bring his sword away without being hit, Imre raised his left arm to take the brunt of the attack and Ebbina's blade was driven all the way through his already wounded forearm. She kicked him in the stomach, sending him reeling backwards, away from the fight. Tarimev saw the duel and took the opportunity to strike as well. He was able to slice Ebbina across her shin, and she fell to her knees. Tarimev approached her, ready to strike her down, when she looked up at him and said, "My love, would you really kill me?"

He paused. Looking into her eyes he could see the eyes of the real Ebbina and not those of a dark apparition, and he found unable to bring himself to finish the fight. She smiled weakly, "You cannot take the life of someone you love, Tarimev."

Tarimev hesitated for another moment, then he lowered his weapon. Watching what was unfolding, Imre shouted, "Finish it, Tarimev. She isn't real."

"No," Tarimev replied in a monotone voice, "I will not kill her."

Imre struggled to his feet and weakly tried to

stumble over to Tarimev, "She's only an illusion."

"How can I believe you?" Tarimev asked. "Just because you say so, does not mean it is true."

Imre shook his head, "She's in your head." He picked up a small rock from the floor and threw it at Tarimev. It hit him square in the head, knocking him back to his senses.

Tarimev stared at Ebbina, still kneeling on the floor, and drove his sword deep into her chest. His eyes filled with tears as she burst into light, and she disappeared, fully releasing Tarimev from her spell.

Tarimev untucked his undershirt and tore some fabric away from it, and he handed it to Imre who tied it around his wounded forearm. He then cut some more fabric away and tied it around his head to stem the bleeding from his eye. The two men looked at each other, and silently made their way up the stairs at the far end of the room.

22

Torvald looked through his wardrobe and picked out his nicest set of finery, got dressed and went next door, to Princess Cayte's room. He knocked on the door and waited for a reply. It didn't take long for her to answer She was standing in front of Torvald wearing a red ball gown with a blue sash across the waist. The top was low-cut on her chest but not very revealing, and it fit her body perfectly. She had left her short hair loose just above her shoulders. She wore a diamond necklace and a matching tiara atop her head, and it shimmered in the sun as if it were made of pure light.

"You look beautiful," Torvald said, beaming with pride.

"Thank you," she replied as she gave him a kiss on the cheek before turning away from him to put on shoes that matched.

"Are you ready to go?" he asked. She offered her

hand to him and they walked out of the room. They walked downstairs to the ballroom and stood in front of the door. They linked arms together and the two guards outside the room pushed the double door open for them. As they stepped into the room a servant announced them, "Her Highness, Princess Cayte of Worthervir, and Sir Torvald Storheam."

The place instantly went quiet. Torvald could feel his heart beating faster than it ever did when he was in combat. He glanced around at those there, and all eyes were upon them. This was the first time that they had attended an official event as a couple. Everyone knew that they were together, even the most diehard supporters of Princess Cayte's father had to be wondering what this meant for their beliefs now that she was seen in public with her own bodyguard.

It didn't take long for the crowd to start muttering amongst themselves. Torvald kept his head high and they walked to the royal table at the head of the room, and took their seats. The King stood from his seat and addressed the crowd, "I thank you all for coming today. Before we begin, I would like to dedicate this ball to the engagement of Princess Cayte and Sir Torvald. Would you both please stand?"

They obliged, and were greeted with applause and cheers for both of them. Torvald glanced over at Cayte who was smiling radiantly, her cheeks were flushed and she had tears in her eyes. The King continued, "It is my pleasure to introduce to you all the future Queen and King of Worthervir. With this in mind, Sir Torvald Storheam shall henceforth be known as His Royal Highness, Prince Torvald."

He sat down once again and the musicians began to

play on harps, flutes and violins. It wasn't long until the ballroom floor filled up with couples and the dancing began. "Do you want to dance?" Torvald asked.

"Yes!" Cayte said excitedly. Her smile widened as the two of them made their way to the other dancers.

They danced for hours, and Torvald couldn't help but notice how Cayte held onto him tightly and enjoyed every moment of being close with him. After another song ended, they returned to where they had been sitting. Torvald leaned back against his chair and took a deep breath. He watched as the people continued to dance around the room.

Cayte smiled at him and rested her head on his shoulder, "I love your strength and courage. You are everything that I never knew I needed."

Torvald turned towards her and kissed her gently on the lips.

As Tarimev and Imre climbed the stairs, they could see a bright light at the top. They continued climbing and began to feel strong winds blowing through the opening. When they reached the top, they knew that they wear nearing the mountain's summit. They were on a plateau of the mountain, but they couldn't see far because of the clouds surrounding them. In the distance, there was the slight flickering of two torches.

"That must be the way we need to go," Tarimev said.

Imre nodded and they headed off in the direction of the torches.

They got nearer to the lights and could make out the figures of two creatures standing next to each other. Both figures were at least seven feet tall, broad and muscular, and both holding a torch. One figure had four arms, the other only two.

"Can you see that?" Imre whispered.

Tarimev nodded, "What are they? They look too big to be human."

"The one seems to have four arms; I only know of one bipedal creature with four arms. The Gliss."

"What about the other one?"

"I don't know. We have to go that way though, they must be guarding something." Imre said as he started sneaking towards the figures.

They neared the pair and stopped once they could see them. The one with four arms was indeed a Gliss as Imre had identified. It was an immense beast, covered in black fur with an ursine face and four arms. It was holding a club with its upper right hand and wearing animal skins. The second figure was slightly taller, with dark green skin and no hair. It wore fur-trimmed trousers and had a leather harness on its chest. In its hands were a large halberd. It was grinding its jaw, with sharp tusks sticking out of its mouth. Tarimev had never seen one in person, seeing as they had been extinct for nearly eighty years, but he knew from paintings that he was looking at an Orc. He was aware of the history of the race; the Orcs were known for being fearsome warriors and in the Orcish War they withheld attacks from the combined might of the entire world for over thirty years. As Tarimev stared at it, he heard Sivik's words ring through his head, "They will return, there will be war." It seemed like he finally knew who, or rather what, was returning.

"We have to fight *those*," Imre said in shock.

Tarimev nodded. "I think you should use your magic; they don't seem to know we are here yet so we can surprise them."

Imre looked at the creatures closely. "I'll give it my all." He drew his sword and ignited the blade. As soon as his blade caught light the two creatures could see his silhouette through the fog. They dropped their torches and bared their teeth, before roaring and charging towards the two men.

The royal ball continued into the night, and a handful of the guests were still enjoying themselves. Many had left the palace or retired to the guest rooms as the night had grown late. A few couples remained at the dance floor, including the two newly engaged royals.

Torvald and Cayte were dancing slowly when Cayte pulled away from him and stared deeply into his eyes. She wrapped her arms around him and held him tight, "When we get married, I want to see the world. We should take a long trip around all the nations and then finally settle down in the palace."

"That sounds perfect. I would love to travel the world with you."

She kissed him tenderly on the cheek, "And then we will have children and live happily ever after."

Torvald laughed and said, "There's time for that yet, we are still young. I still have a career ahead of me."

Cayte giggled and kissed him again, "But you are already doing so well, I wouldn't mind if you decided to retire early."

Torvald thought she was joking and laughed as he

held her close.

"You're not serious," he said as he kissed her.

She pulled back and looked at him, "I'm dead serious. I'll need you by my side when I'm Queen."

Torvalds brow furrowed, and he raised his voice slightly, "Then I'll retire when you take the throne, but until then I have trained too hard to retire now. I discussed this with your father earlier and he said it wouldn't be an issue."

Cayte shook her head, "You discussed it with him before me?"

Torvald nodded, "Yes, we had a drink together earlier and he asked if I was worried about the marriage."

Cayte smiled, "That was the only thing you could think of that worried you?"

"Of course, I can't wait to start a life with you. I just don't want to forgo my duty as a knight."

Cayte nuzzled into his shoulder, "No, you shouldn't worry. I'm sorry, we'll work it out as we go along, but I won't stop you from living your life. I love you, Torvald."

Torvald sighed and hugged her close, "I love you too, Cayte. Thank you for understanding."

The two danced for a while longer, holding each other closely as they enjoyed the moment.

The barbarous creatures charged towards their enemies, weapons aloft. Imre launched a fireball at the orc and managed to hit it squarely in the chest. But it was barely slowed by the strike and swung its halberd at Imre, who quickly jumped aside. Upon landing, he saw the orc's club pass inches from his head. His breath came out in a deep sigh as he watched the orc continue to approach him, "This is bad..." he thought to himself. At the same time, the Gliss reached Tarimev and smashed its club into his side. Taken by surprise, he lost his balance and fell to the ground with a loud thud.

The orc swung its halberd down at Imre, who raised his blade to block it. He held his sword with both hands, struggling to push back against the brute strength of the creature with his wounded arm. He focused his magic and sent a burst of fire from his sword, pushing the orc back just enough for him to roll away and leap back onto his feet.

A growl escaped the orc's lips as it tried to regain its footing, "You are strong, warrior!"

Imre nodded and said, "I should hope so." He ran forwards, cutting his sword through the air in front of him as he advanced. The orc roared and swung its halberd, but Imre easily dodged the attack and rolled under its legs. He kept running and launched a fireball at the Gliss ahead of him, just as it was about to bring its club down onto Tarimev. The blast hit the Gliss in the chest, making it fall backwards to the ground.

Imre helped his friend to his feet as Tarimev nodded, "Thank you, I owe you one."

They glanced over at the orc, who was walking towards the two men, snarling.

"Stay on the Gliss, I've got the orc," Imre shouted as he ran towards the orc again. Tarimev looked back at the Gliss as it began to lumber forward. He planted his feet and placed a second hand on his sword, holding it beside himself ready to swing. With only one eye, he was struggling to gauge how far away it was.

He took a guess and swung his sword in a wide arc, hoping to land a blow on the beast.

Tarimev's blade cut through the air and lightly grazed the chest of his foe, barely enough to even cut its skin. The Gliss didn't seem fazed by the simple wound, it raised its club and brought it down at Tarimev with anger in its eyes. Tarimev blocked the strike with his sword, and rammed his shoulder into the gliss's stomach, knocking it back a few steps. "Sod it," Tarimev shouted as he ripped his makeshift bandage away from his eye. The vision in his left eye was marred with a blood-red tint, yet he had regained his perception of depth. He spun his sword round in his hand, and charged towards the Gliss.

King Occime was seated at the head table, watching as the ball drew to a close, "It has been an honour to host this ball," he said to his gathered guests. The guests bowed their heads in appreciation.

"Please join me in congratulating Princess Cayte and Prince Storheam one more time."

The guests applauded once again as the pair waved. It seemed that the crowd were rather pleased with the outcome, judging by the cheers ringing around the room.

As the celebration came to a close, Torvald and Cayte made their way out of the ballroom. Before they got through the door, Torvald heard his name shouted from behind him. He turned to see his father standing there, his face reddened from drinking and his speech slurred.

"Well done son! You have elevated our family to even greater heights than me. Maybe you aren't such a waste of space after all. Look at the power you've won for our family."

Torvald scoffed, "I didn't fall in love with Cayte for power. I don't care about being King so much as being with her."

Elmont laughed, "Nonsense, you can do great things for us now. Take care of us like we took care of you."

"Took care of me? When was that?" Torvald asked, anger and venom seeping into his words.

"When you were born! Look at you, you're healthy as a horse and better looking than most of those nobles."

Torvald smiled, "Then you handed me off to a nanny and travelled the world to make yourself rich. The only time I saw you was when you beat me as punishment for whatever you were told I did wrong. Is this what you meant by taking care of me?"

"That wasn't my fault," Elmont protested.

"No, of course not," Torvald replied sarcastically. His father scowled and balled his fist, "You ungrateful bastard!"

"Father, stop it, you know as well as I do that it's true," Torvald said firmly. Elmont shook his head and punched Torvald in the jaw. Torvald fell to the floor, the punch sending searing pain through his head. Elmont took advantage of his weakened position and kicked him in the ribs.

"Get up! Get up or you'll be sorry!" Elmont screamed. Cayte screamed and tried to pull Elmont away, but he hit her away with the back of his hand. She staggered back and fell hard onto the floor.

Elmont was grabbed by two guards who began to

drag him away. "You're under arrest for attacking the Princess of Worthervir. Come with us now."

A commotion broke out amongst the guests as they all realised what happened to Cayte. The guards dragged Elmont towards the exit as he screamed objections. Torvald pulled himself up and then helped Cayte to her feet. He could hear his father shouting insults and curses at him and decided to follow him out.

"What are you doing? Let the guards handle it," Cayte whispered.

"He hit you," Torvald replied with anger in his voice. He quickly caught up to the guards, grabbed his father's shoulder and yanked him around, out of the grip of the guards. He headbutted his father in the face, and Elmont's nose burst with blood. Torvald pushed his father to the ground, kicked him in the face and yelled at the guards, "What are you waiting for? Get him out of here!"

The guards nodded and hoisted Elmont up from under his arms. They dragged him away and Torvald watched as they got to the end of the corridor.

Torvald felt a hand on his shoulder and turned to see Cayte looking worried.

"Are you alright?" she asked.

Torvald's eyes began to water and he sobbed into Cayte's shoulder. "I don't know what came over me. He neglected me my whole childhood and just beat me instead of parenting."

Cayte embraced him tightly. "Let it go. You've got it out of you now. It's not your fault."

Torvald sniffed and wiped his tears away, "I'm sorry. I must seem so weak right now."

"You're not weak. You're the strongest man I know." She kissed him on the cheek again "Come on, let's get you to bed."

Torvald nodded and followed Cayte out of the ballroom and towards her chambers.

Tarimev slashed at the Gliss, whilst dodging blows from its clawed arms. He needed to find some way to defeat the creature before he ended up dead. Tarimev ducked underneath another swipe from the Gliss and landed a cut on its side. Blood sprayed across the stone mountaintop, staining it red with gore.

He had to keep moving, otherwise, his foe would catch him. He stabbed at his enemy's stomach but the Gliss sidestepped the attack and grabbed Tarimev's throat, lifting him in to the air. Tarimev shouted and kicked his legs wildly but couldn't free himself. The Gliss tightened its grip and Tarimev's vision began to blur.

Imre was engaged in a duel with the orc, each of their weapons clashing against each other and neither able to get the upper hand. Imre swung his sword, aiming to cut through the orc's neck, but the orc blocked the attack. Imre defended himself against the orc's next strike, then dashed away from the orc's reach and shot another fireball toward the Gliss from his left hand.

The Gliss dropped Tarimev and he fell to the ground, coughing and gasping for breath. He lay there and looked up at the Gliss, which was recovering from the burn on its arm. He had managed to keep a hold of his sword, and raised it up at the Gliss.

"Kill me now, monster. End this once and for all,"

Tarimev cried.

The Gliss stepped forward and swung its claws down at Tarimev, who rolled out of the way and jumped to his feet. The Gliss bellowed and lashed out again, trying to slash at Tarimev's face. Tarimev dodged the claws and then swung his blade at the gliss's leg. The Gliss howled as the sword pierced its thigh and tried to stomp on Tarimev, but he avoided the attack.

The Gliss roared, falling to one knee before it swung its club at Tarimev again, but he stepped back and avoided the attack. He stepped forward to attack when the Gliss lashed out with its claws and left deep cuts in his armour.

Tarimev stumbled backwards slightly from the strike. He plunged his sword into the chest of the creature, then wrenched the blade from side to side, slicing through the Gliss' flesh. The creature struggled, but Tarimev held on to his sword tight and watched as the life drained from his opponent's body. He took a step back and the Gliss fell to a heap on the ground. The creature twitched and its limbs convulsed before it finally stopped moving.

Tarimev breathed a sigh of relief and wiped his blade clean.

Imre charged at the orc, once more, this time succeeding in stabbing his sword into the orc's side. The orc bellowed and swiped at Imre's face with his halberd. Imre dodged the attack, but the orc was surprisingly quick for its size, and came at him again. The two fighters clashed weapons together, sending sparks flying in the air. Imre parried the orc's strikes and spun away, trying to get some space between them. He moved around the orc and looked for an opening in its defences. He saw his chance when the orc lifted its halberd and prepared another swing. Imre summoned a fireball in his left hand and threw it.

It hit the creature square in the chest, knocking it off balance. Imre leaped at the orc, thrusting his sword up under the orc's chin and into its brain. The orc slumped to the ground and Imre withdrew his sword. He let out a grunt of exertion and turned to see Tarimev standing over the lifeless corpse of the Gliss. He sheathed his sword and his eyes faded back to their natural blue colour.

Tarimev walked over to the orc and kicked it once, watching as blood gushed out of the wound in its head. He glanced at Imre who was staring at him with concern.

"Are you alright?"

Tarimev nodded and sheathed his sword.

"I'm fine, Imre. But how in the name of all the gods is a fucking orc still alive?"

Imre shrugged and looked down at the orc. "I don't know. It's worrying though, orcs only live about seventy years. Even if this one was born at the end of the war, he would still be past his lifespan by now."

Tarimev shook his head. "We need to see what they were guarding and find out what's going on here."

They walked to the side of the mountain where the two creatures were first stood. There, they found a wooden door embedded into the rock, and Tarimev pushed it open with a loud creak. The pair walked inside and found themselves in a large circular room, lit by torches on either side of the walls. The room was cold, colder than Tarimev had ever felt before, and it made his skin prickle. In the centre of the room was a large font, full of a viscous, red liquid. Tarimev stared at the font for a moment, unsure of what he was looking at, though he had seen it many times before.

"Blood," Imre stated with an air of certainty, "Well if we weren't sure before, we are now. There's a necromancer in this mountain."

Tarimev approached a door on the far end of the room, and the sound of footsteps echoed from behind it. He turned to Imre.

"Through here," he whispered. He pushed the door as carefully as he could to stop it from making a sound, and opened it quickly when he heard nothing. The room beyond was a study, carved out of the stone and illuminated by the same green glow he saw before. Bookshelves lined the walls, filled with scrolls. Hunched over a stone altar, was a tall figure, cloaked in black robes and a hood covered their head. Tarimev and Imre entered the room, swords drawn, ready to fight. A low growl escaped the cloaked figure's lips, and they both froze.

The dark-robed figure slowly rose from its hunched position and turned towards them, revealing their features; green skin with a grey tinge, tusks sticking out of its mouth, and a thick white beard with a braid down the centre.

"You disturb me," the figure hissed, eyes glowing emerald green with anger.

23

Torvald sat in an armchair in one of the rooms in Cayte's chambers. His clothing was loosened, and he had brandy in his hand as he waited for Cayte to change out of her ballgown. The room was warm from a fire that burned in the hearth beside him, and he had been admiring the evening sky through the window in front of him when he heard Cayte approach from behind. He looked over his shoulder at her. She was wearing a simple white nightgown that clung tightly to her body, and she carried herself with a certain confidence that Torvald found appealing. Her face still bore a red mark from Elmont's strike.

"I am sorry for how things went tonight. I should have expected my father to be himself," Torvald said as he took a drink from his glass.

Cayte shook her head. "Don't blame yourself for what happened. You did what you had to."

"I did more than I should have," Torvald said. He put down his glass and placed his head in his hands. "I made an enemy of my family tonight."

Cayte walked over to where Torvald was standing and took hold of his shoulders.

"You will make enemies no matter what you do." She looked him in the eyes. "You gave him less than he deserved. And you protected me."

"I suppose you're right about that," Torvald said as Cayte bent down and kissed him on the lips. Then she took a seat on his lap.

"He will face a trial for hitting me, but I will speak to my father and delay it until after our wedding. He will remain in a cell until then. He won't torment you anymore, my love."

"Thank you," Torvald said softly.

They sat together in silence for several minutes before Torvald finally broke the quiet. "It is strange how we got here so quickly. It seems like only yesterday that I was a recruit, nervous about meeting a princess for the first time. Now you're about to become my wife."

"And I am happy to be your bride," Cayte said, smiling at him.

"You're the best thing that ever happened to me," Torvald said, as he took another sip of brandy and sank comfortably to sleep in the armchair, the love of his life in his arms.

Tarimev and Imre stood opposite the robed beast. It looked at them with venom in its eyes and spoke again in the common language of Lotine.

"Who are you that disrupts my rituals?" it asked.

Imre looked at the orc in fear, "Who are you, creature?"

The creature snorted derisively, "You may call me Throkin. Chief Wizard of the Orcs."

Tarimev stared at the creature, trying to determine whether or not this was some type of trick. "The Orcs are dead. Your people were hunted to extinction at the end of the war. There were no survivors."

Throkin looked at Imre and then turned back to Tarimev, "So they say, but there are always survivors." He walked over to a table and picked up a globe. "The world is larger than you know. Much bigger than any of us can imagine. Our leader sent troops far and wide in search of a place to settle. When we came upon our home, we thought it perfect. It was wild and untouched by the hands of man."

"You mean to say that your people have been hiding since the war?" Imre asked.

"Yes. We've been building our forces, preparing to take back our ancestral lands from the invaders. And I'm afraid that I can't let you two expose these long-formed plans before we are ready to reveal ourselves to the world."

Tarimev stepped forward, drawing his sword, "You cannot stop us from revealing the truth."

Throkin drew his hood back and bared his teeth at Tarimev. "You know nothing of our magic. If you try anything foolish, I will simply kill you and use your bones to call forth the spirits that will form my army."

Tarimev kept his blade pointed at Throkin, "I am afraid that I cannot leave here without killing you."

"Then you must die," Throkin said as he summoned a green skull in the palm of his hand. He began chanting in a foreign tongue. As he chanted, the skull began to crackle and smoke.

Throkin threw the skull at Tarimev who jumped to the side, narrowly avoiding the projectile. The skull exploded against the wall behind Tarimev, knocking him forwards and off his feet.

As Tarimev fell to the floor, Throkin raised both his hands and two skeletons grew upwards from the ground, surrounded by the same green mist that Tarimev and Imre had seen throughout the mountain. One approached Tarimev, and the other Imre. Tarimev didn't have time to react and he found himself grabbed by the throat and lifted into the air. He flailed his legs as he was lifted off the ground, attempting to free himself from the grip of the skeletal warrior.

Imre tried to move towards Tarimev, but a skeleton blocked his path. He could see Throkin watching with a smirk on his face.

"There's nothing left to do now," Throkin said. "You both will die here, and I hope that your remains will enjoy serving the Orcish Empire."

Tarimev struggled to breathe as the skeletal warrior squeezed tighter around his neck.

"Damn you!" Tarimev shouted. "Let go of me! You monster!"

Throkin laughed, "Your death is already written. Your gods have abandoned you."

The skeleton threw Tarimev across the room and he collided with the wall, causing him to slump to the ground, his sword falling from his grip. Imre watched in horror as both skeletal warriors now approached him. He readied his sword and magic and braced for the assault. The skeletons reached down to their waists, and the green mist surrounding them formed into swords in their hands. They moved to attack Imre, and he created a wall of flame between himself and the creatures. But they crossed through the flames like it was nothing and continued their approach towards the Marçhal.

Imre planted his feet and prepared to defend himself. He could feel the wound on his arm burning as the skeletons got closer. His magic began to weaken, and the flames flowing through him lessened. A sense of hopelessness washed over him as his magic failed. The skeletons got close enough to strike and he swung his sword at one of the creatures, hoping to make it drop its weapon. Instead, he struck the creature in the head, and the creature collapsed to the floor. The second skeleton managed to swing its sword at Imre, but he was able to dodge out of the way and deflect the blow. The remaining skeleton lunged forward and swung its sword at Imre. He leaped backwards and the skeleton missed him completely. It was too slow to recover and Imre brought his sword around and hit it in the chest, shattering the bone structure and ending its life. As the bones hit the floor, both skeletons crumbled to dust and the green mist dissipated.

The night hadn't even reached its midpoint, yet Torvald had awoken in his seat, Cayte still slumbering on his lap, leaving him alone with his thoughts. He sat with his arms around her, staring blankly ahead. The fire crackled and spit sparks as it burned in the fireplace, throwing dancing shadows across the walls.

He carefully lifted Cayte and carried her to his bed before leaving the room. He walked down the grand staircase and exited the castle. He saw several soldiers patrolling the grounds, each one bowing to him as he passed. He knew it would take a while for him to get used to being treated as a member of the royal family but he did not mind being addressed with respect.

Torvald made his way into the city and walked through the streets until he came across a tavern in the Old Dock Ward. He entered and took a seat at the bar. After a moment, the bartender came over and placed a glass next to him, "What'll it be?"

"Just an ale," Torvald replied.

He immediately sipped at his drink when the bartender brought it over and looked around the room. There were only a few other patrons present. Most of them appeared to be sailors or merchants, and they all seemed to be speaking in hushed tones. As he enjoyed his drink, he heard someone approaching and turned to see an old man standing next to him.

"Excuse me, me and my friends were just talking about you," the old man said.

"About me?" Torvald asked.

"Yes. We are sure we recognise you, but we don't know where from," the man said.

"I'm a knight, you must have seen me around the city," Torvald replied.

"Ah yes, I must've done," the old man said. "You aren't the fellow that saved Grazan from those money lenders, are you?"

"That's right," Torvald said. "You know Grazan?"

"Yes, he's my son-in-law," the old man said. "Come join us for a drink. It's on me."

As the old man led Torvald to his table, his friends joined them as well.

"This is Harnen, Ghent and Denton, I am Sira." the old man said. "Gentlemen, this is the knight that helped Grazan."

"It's nice to meet you," Torvald said.

They all clinked glasses and sipped their drinks in unison.

"What brings you here?" Sira asked.

"I needed some time away from the palace," Torvald replied. "My duties haven't been easy recently. I thought a change of scenery might be good for me."

The old man smiled and nodded, "I can understand. My father was a knight, and he struggled with his duty a lot, but he always gave his best. So many people looked up to him and he never let them down."

They continued chatting for a while, and Torvald learned that all three men had fathers who were knights during the Orcish War. Eventually, the conversation turned to the final days of the war when the Orcs were wiped out at the Battle of Maugr.

"I'll never forget the stories," Harnen said. "I was only a child, but I heard them countless times when the soldiers returned home. They tell tales of how the Orc King was killed by a single arrow, and the final orc tribe was destroyed in a matter of hours."

"We were lucky to win," Ghent added.

"I always heard that the battle wasn't as glorious as we were told. Apparently, it was more like an execution than anything else. And there were fewer orcs in the city than were expected." Denton said.

Sira nodded, "I heard the same. They were

expecting a force of thousands, but only a couple of hundred elderly orcs remained."

Torvald shook his head, "A few hundred? What about the warriors?"

"I don't think they ever found any sign of them," Denton said.

Sira tapped his finger against the table, "There are rumours that a group of warriors escaped and fled to the ocean."

Harnen roared with laughter, "You sound like crazy people. I'm going home before I catch your insanity."

The three men all agreed and stood to leave. They shook Torvald's hand in turn and left him to finish his drink; once he had, he realised he had drunk more than he realised, enraptured as he was by the conversation with his drinking companions. He staggered out of the tavern and through the streets back towards the palace. He reached the Palace District and was greeted by guards as he entered the grounds. The guard opened the gate for him and Torvald thanked him but didn't pay attention to his words, instead he was focused on keeping upright. He stopped to lean against the gatepost to steady himself. The guard leaned close and said, "Your Highness, perhaps you should get to bed, you're not looking too well."

Torvald smiled and shook his head. "I'll be fine, thank you though."

He staggered up the path to the palace door and entered. It was dark and he stumbled through the corridors, keeping one hand on the wall to stop himself from falling until he made it to his chambers. He had no candles lit so he fumbled around in the dark looking for his bed. Once he had found it, he collapsed onto the soft mattress and fell asleep.

Tarimev struggled to his feet, his whole body aching from hitting the wall. He was getting used to the aches and pains by now, but it still wasn't a pleasant feeling. As he stood, he saw Imre strike down the skeletons. He picked his sword back up off the floor and faced Throkin. Imre joined Tarimev by his side, his sword barely flickering with embers. "Nice of you to re-join me," Imre said with a smirk.

"Better late than never," Tarimev replied.

Throkin's face contorted with anger, "ENOUGH! I'll deal with you myself. I look forward to crushing your skulls!" He started towards the two men, his eyes rolling back in his head and turning black. He summoned an axe in each hand with his magic. Tarimev and Imre both positioned themselves with their swords ahead of them, preparing to fight.

Throkin's mouth opened wide and he breathed out black fog on the two men. The smoke swirled around them and suddenly they were surrounded by a cloud of black fog. Tarimev couldn't see anything beyond the mist except the faint embers of Imre's sword. He could hear footsteps approaching him, and began to see a green glow approaching him through the fog. A green axe struck down towards him through the fog and Throkin roared. Tarimev dodged to his left and swung his blade across. His sword connected with the axe, knocking it away.

Imre stepped forward and swung his blade at Throkin, but the orc stepped back into the fog and the blow missed its target. Seconds later Throkin struck again, this time towards Imre. He slashed both axes towards the Marçhal, who defended the first strike with his blade. The second axe came quicker than expected and drove deep into Imre's left shoulder. He screamed in pain, and when he did flames exploded out of him, clearing the fog from the room.

Throkin stepped back in shock and fear, his hands loosening their grips on his axes, and as they fell to the floor, they faded into nothing. Imre readied a fireball and launched it at Throkin. The orc deflected the shot with his own magic and went to throw a shot back of his own when Imre shot another attack. He threw fireball after fireball, fuelled by nothing more than rage and pain. Throkin was forced backwards as he tried in vain to defend himself. Tarimev watched the barrage of attacks on the orc and took advantage of it. He broke into a run and dove at Throkin, wrapping his arms around his waist to tackle him to the ground. They rolled across the floor but Throkin used his great strength to pin Tarimev to the ground, where he rained blows down at him with his fists.

Tarimev struggled with everything he had trying to break free, but Throkin's weight held him firm. He felt himself weakening under the orc's attacks. Watching the fight, Imre sheathed his sword and raised both of his arms up, summoning chains of fire in the air above his palms. He threw them at Throkin's arms and they wrapped around his wrists, their weight dragging the orc backwards and pinning him to the wall. The burning chains seared into Throkin's flesh, sending the orc into a rage as he tried to break free, to no avail. Tarimev approached the beast, and slid his sword slowly along Throkin's throat, slicing it open just enough for blood to begin pouring out. Tarimev drove his sword into Throkin's stomach and wrenched it about, before pulling the blade free and placing it back in its scabbard.

Throkin let out a weak roar of pain, then slumped forward, lifeless. Tarimev stood in front of the corpse, breathing heavily. He looked at Imre who was using his magic to cauterise his wounds. Imre winced as he cast a small plume of flames at his forearm, which quickly healed over, leaving just a faint scar.

Tarimev began looking around on the nearby table, to see what Throkin had left behind. He found a sheaf of papers, and upon opening them he saw a neatly hand-written letter. He read it to himself:

Throkin,

My plans are coming along. I have struck a bargain with the Gliss tribes for them to aid us in our invasion. Once you have finished with your part of the plan, I want you to bring your army back to the Black Crater to meet our allies. We are ready to attack upon your return, we have enough warriors to invade now but we will wait for your additions to our force.

The Gliss who brought this message is now in your service and will aid you in your experiments. I expect a response soon informing me of your progress.

Kradak

Tarimev noticed there was another letter on the table next to where the papers were stacked. He picked it up and read it. It appeared to be the response to the one he had just put down.

Overlord Kradak,

The Trials of Knights

My greatest apologies that it's taking longer than we planned, but it can't be helped. The corpses that I have been able to work with so far have been too decomposed to be viable warriors. I am currently attempting to restore the damaged bodies but, as you know yourself, once the flesh begins to rot it is very difficult to repair. It is not an easy tas

The letter stopped suddenly, and the ink still seemed wet. Tarimev realised that Throkin must have still been writing it when they disturbed him. Tarimev silently handed the letters to Imre, who read through them. He nodded and handed them back. "Take these to your king and inform him of the threat. I will inform my order." Imre said. He picked up a bronze cube off the table, which was decorated with many different runes. "Take this to your court sorcerer. It is a sorcerer's message box; messages can be stored inside that only another sorcerer can access. I would take it to the Marçhals but I fear they would hide this information away from the nations."

"I'll do it," Tarimev replied, "but shouldn't you take some proof with you?"

Imre drew his sword and in one movement sliced Throkin's head from his body. He picked up the head and wrapped it in some cloth he found nearby before hanging it from his shoulder like a bag. "That should be enough to prove that the orcs have returned."

The two men left the room and retraced their steps back through the mountain. The tasks they faced on the way up had vanished and they were simply walking through empty stone rooms. Tarimev wondered how they had managed to escape the place alive. They passed through several other chambers, each more silent than the last, until finally, after what felt like hours, they reached the exit of the mountain. The sun was basking the rocks in a warm orange glow as it set, and both Tarimev and Imre took a deep breath, finally free of the stale air inside the mountain. "We should walk until nightfall, get into the forest and camp for the night before returning to Qoan." Tarimev said, pointing to the northern forest.

They walked for a while but the forest was silent and still. As the light faded further, they made their way deeper into the trees and eventually found a clearing with a small stream running through it. They could hear the water splashing against the rocks, and birds chirping in the branches above them. They sat down by the river to rest and ate the last of their dried meat before drifting off to a well-earned sleep.

24

Torvald was awoken from his groggy sleep by the sound of hammering on his door. He stumbled out of bed and threw open the door to find a palace guard waiting for him. The guard spoke first, "Good Morning, Your Highness. King Occime and Marçhal Bergan request your attendance at a council meeting within the hour.

"Thank you. Tell them I will be there as soon as I am dressed."

The guard nodded and closed the door behind him as Torvald hurried to put his clothes on. He put on his underclothing and armour on top, then fastened his sword to his waist before leaving his room. As he walked down the castle hallways, he felt like every eye in the palace was upon him. He was certain that after his actions with his father, and his engagement to the princess, he would be the talk of the city for days to come.

He made it through the palace without incident and found himself outside the doors to the war room where the king and his advisors would be waiting. As he entered the room all the men, except the King, stood from the table at attention. Torvald bowed to the King as he walked forward into the middle of the room. He took his seat beside King Occime and the other men all sat back down around the table. All eyes turned toward the King, "Welcome Prince Torvald, thank you for joining us. We have much to discuss today but before we begin, let me remind everyone that this is a private meeting and no one else is to enter or listen in until after the meeting has ended. Marçhal, would you care to start?"

Marçhal Bergan stood up from the table and looked around the room before saying, "As I am sure you are aware by now, the recruit Tarimev Riswaell was sent to the Yevanti Wilds in pursuit of a suspected necromancer." Torvald perked up at the mention of his old friend, worried about what news he was about to hear.

"Unfortunately, we have not yet received any news from Riswaell himself," Bergan continued, "but, as every morning, I performed some rituals earlier and I am detecting no signs of dark magic from the Ashen Mountain region. At least none that would indicate a necromancer is present. I believe that Riswaell has succeeded in his quest, but we will not know for certain until he returns."

Torvald was pleased to hear this news; he hadn't thought of his friend these past few days with everything that had been going on in his own life, but he couldn't wait to see Tarimev again. Occime spoke next, "That is good to hear. If Riswaell returns with positive news then we will not only give him a pardon for his crime, but also offer him his knighthood. He is a good knight, and a good man."

"I agree with the King," Sergeant Koln added, "Riswaell is a loyal soldier and he deserves our gratitude for his hard work. Especially if he has successfully made contact with the Yevanti."

The conversation continued and they discussed many other topics before finally coming to the end of their meeting. The King dismissed everyone except Torvald. "I would like you to meet me in the throne room an hour after noon, please."

Torvald bowed and said, "Of course."

He left the war room and went for breakfast.

It was nearing noon when Tarimev and Imre stepped through the wooden gates of Qoan. The two friends were both tired from their challenges over the past few days but still happy to be back. Tarimev almost felt as though he was home, despite the fact he had only spent a few days of his life here. As they walked through the main gate, a familiar voice called out to them from behind.

"Yevan! Marçhal!"

They turned to see Prince Hodrin walking toward them from the woods, a boar slung over his shoulder and a bloody spear in his hand. Hodrin approached them, dropped the boar and stabbed his spear into the ground. He hugged them both before speaking, "I take it you finished your quest?"

"I did, but it was quite tough I tell you." Tarimev

replied, "But I have returned intact so I count it successful."

Hodrin nodded. "Well my cousin will be pleased to see you. She has been waiting for your return, not that she would admit that to anyone."

Tarimev felt his face flush with embarrassment. He was excited to see Ebbina again, but he didn't want it to be a public spectacle.

"I should go inside and greet her," Tarimev said, looking toward the gates.

Hodrin smiled and said, "Yes, of course. Go. "

Tarimev turned to leave when Imre stopped him. "I will leave you here, my friend. I have to get back to the Marçhal Citadel and tell them what we have found. It has been good to see you, and I hope our paths cross again soon."

Tarimev pulled Imre into a hug and slapped him on the back, "Me too, Imre."

Tarimev watched as his friend walked away and then started to make his way to the Great Hall.

As Tarimev walked through town he saw people strolling around, going about their daily business. Some waved hello to him as he passed by while others stared at him from a distance. Most of the townspeople recognized him as the Yevan that had saved the tribe. It didn't take long to reach the Great Hall of Qoan where he could see Ebbina sitting on her wooden throne, talking to a group of people. She spotted Tarimev approaching and started smiling broadly.

"Yevan! Welcome back," she shouted to him. She dismissed the people around her and stood from her throne.

The Trials of Knights

Ebbina looked more beautiful than Tarimev remembered her. Her hair was styled differently, all gathered into a single braid which fell over her left shoulder. Her injuries from Eshami were fading, but even with the bruises her beauty shone through.

As he approached Ebbina, she placed a hand on his arm and leaned in close. "I'm happy to see you," she whispered to him.

Tarimev blushed and thanked her. "You look lovelier than I remember," he said.

She laughed at his comment and said, "Thank you. How did it go?"

"We defeated the dark wizard. It was quite a task, but we just about made it."

Ebbina smiled as she looked into his eyes before her face fell and tears welled up in her eyes. "Oh no," she said, "what happened?"

Tarimev explained the fight against the apparitions, how they were people he cared about, and how the apparition of her wounded his eye.

"Are you okay? Are you hurt anywhere else?" Ebbina asked worriedly.

"It's sore but I can still see. And my shoulder was hurt, but it will heal in time."

Ebbina took his hands in hers and said, "Of all the people you care about in the world, it was me that appeared in front of you?"

Tarimev smiled at her and shook his head. "I don't think I would've liked any of the others much better," he told her with a smile.

Ebbina's' smile grew wider and she kissed him gently on the cheek. "Do you have to return to Alerill? Can't you stay here in Qoan?"

Tarimev nodded, "Yes, I do. I have to tell them what has happened. But I will return as often as I can, just to see you."

"Take this then," she said as she removed a pendant from around her neck. It was golden with a small ruby in the centre, "I will want this back."

She handed him the necklace and he put it around his neck. She kissed him deeply once more before saying, "Will you at least stay for a meal before you leave?"

Tarimev smiled, "Yes, that would be wonderful."

"Good," she replied, "Join me for a drink while we wait for it to be prepared."

Ebbina told one of her servants what she wanted, and then Tarimev and Ebbina retired to her rooms, where they enjoyed each other's company until a knock at the door indicated that their lunch was ready. They ate a feast of roast boar, fish, bread and fruit. Tarimev hadn't realised just how much a few days can make you miss real food. After eating, Tarimev kissed Ebbina once more and he left her side, wishing he could stay longer with her.

The throne room was empty when Torvald arrived. He noticed that at the head of the room, next to the King's throne, were two new thrones, one on either side. He walked up to the new thrones to investigate them; both thrones were slightly smaller than the King's throne, but they were still made of gold with Worthervirian red cushioning. The one to the left of the main throne had a 'C' emblazoned into the back cushion, and the one to the right had a 'T'. As Torvald looked at them, he heard the main doors to the throne room open, and King Occime walked in with Princess Cayte behind him.

Torvald bowed low, "Your Majesty." He walked over to Cayte and kissed her to say hello.

King Occime looked at Torvald and smiled, "You've already seen them then."

"The thrones?" Torvald asked.

"Yes," the king replied, "they are for my daughter and son-in-law."

Torvald's jaw dropped, "You mean..."

"Yes, they are for the two of you."

Cayte's eyes lit up, "Really?" she asked.

Torvald didn't know what to say.

"The two of you will be running this kingdom one day," the King told them, "I was dropped into this position with no idea how to reign, and I don't want you to be in that same position."

Cayte smiled at her father. "Thank you, Your Majesty."

"Come, let's sit down and see what you think," the King said.

All three sat, facing into the hall from their thrones. "Well?" the King asked.

"They're beautiful," Cayte said as she ran her finger along the armrest, "and so comfortable."

"Indeed, they are," the King replied.

"I think they're perfect," Torvald agreed, "but what are we expected to do now?"

"You will attend with me when I take court and hear the people's concerns twice a week, as well as greeting any foreign dignitaries or messengers in this room. Speaking of which, I am holding court in two hours. It will go on until evening, and I would like you both here."

"We'll be there," Torvald assured him.

"Excellent," the King said as he left his throne and the room.

Tarimev had left Qoan shortly after noon. The Yevanti had recovered his horse for him, but he was still exhausted from the ride. After all, he had been riding as fast as possible for eight hours when he saw Alerill on the horizon. He rode through the city streets, taking in the sights and sounds before reaching the palace. He left his horse at the stables and walked through the gardens towards the entrance. He entered the palace into the entrance hall and went to enter the throne room when he was stopped by a guard.

"Court has finished, recruit. Make an appointment with your Sergeant," he told him.

"I need to see the King. Now!" Tarimev demanded.

The guard looked at him, "What do you want?"

"I need to speak with the King."

The guard shrugged, "Sorry, recruit, but the King has already retired for the night. Go and wait in the War Room, I will see if the prince will speak with you."

"Fine, tell him Tarimev Riswaell needs to speak to him," Tarimev growled.

He walked into the war room, and found it empty, so he took a seat at the table and started thinking about who the prince was. He had never heard anything about a Prince of Alerill, but maybe he had been in another nation for a while. His thoughts were interrupted by a voice, "Recruit. You look lost."

Tarimev recognised the voice immediately,

"Torvald? What are you doing here?" he asked as he stood from his chair and hugged his friend.

"I was told you were waiting to see me," Torvald laughed as he returned the hug, "good to see you again."

"You're the Prince of Alerill now?" Tarimev asked, trying not to sound too surprised.

"Got engaged to Cayte yesterday," Torvald replied, "I woke the King when I was told it was you who was here. He is on his way now. And what's this?" Torvald pointed at Tarimev's lion's head pauldron.

"Bestowed to me as part of my new title," Tarimev said, "I was made the Yevan of the Yevanti Tribe by their Queen. Apparently, it makes me nobility within the tribe."

"How can that be?" Torvald asked, "Those people are barbarians, they don't have a concept of nobility."

"The Yevanti are not what we have been told, they are a wonderful people. Once they trust you, there is nobody more friendly or welcoming."

Torvald opened his mouth to speak again, but was stopped by the doors to the war room swinging open. The King came walking in, wearing a plain tunic and trousers and without his sword, clearly having dressed quickly. He was followed by Marçhal Bergan. Tarimev bowed to the King, "Your Majesty."

"Welcome back, Mr Riswaell," Occime said, "I trust you completed your task, although was it necessary to speak to me at such a late hour?"

"I'm afraid so. The good news is that I defeated a dark wizard in the Ashen Mountain," Tarimev said proudly.

"That's excellent news. But I take it there is also

The Trials of Knights

bad news?" the King asked.

"Yes, there is," Tarimev admitted, "The necromancer was an Orc. And he was guarded by another Orc and a Gliss."

"An Orc? Are you sure?" The King asked, his face displaying a look of fear.

"Without a doubt," Tarimev said. He reached into his pack and pulled out the message box and letters that he recovered from the mountain and handed them to the King. Tarimev went on to explain everything that had happened on his quest, making sure to state how well he was treated by the Yevanti and what Throkin told him about the Orcs. The King read the letters then handed the message box to Bergan, "Take this to my sorcerer, and get back as soon as possible. Torvald, fetch the council."

With that, the King dismissed them. Bergan and Torvald left the war room, leaving King Occime alone with Tarimev.

"Hand me your sword," the King said, "and kneel."

Tarimev did as he was instructed. The King held the sword up and looked it over. He smiled, "This will do nicely," he said as he held Tarimev's own sword over his head, "Tarimev Riswaell, do you swear to serve the Kingdom of Alerill and protect all within it?"

"I do," Tarimev said, as stoically as he could manage with how excited he was now feeling.

"I, therefore, knight you, Sir Tarimev Riswaell, Knight of the King's Army of Worthervir. Congratulations Sir Riswaell, I will ensure that your past indiscretions are forgotten, and that today your career starts anew. Head to the armoury, I believe there is some spare Knight's armour there. Put it on and come back here, you should hear what the council has to say."

Tarimev stood and bowed to the King before going to the armoury to change.

The knights in the armoury looked on curiously as he changed his clothes. He put on the Knight's armour, which was a full set of plate armour except for the left forearm guard and pauldron which Tarimev carried over from his previous armour. He felt full of pride as he walked back towards the war room in his new uniform.

"Well, Sir Riswaell," Sergeant Koln said, "King Occime has just told us of your promotion. Congratulations, it is well deserved."

"Thank you, Sergeant," Tarimev said.

"Now let us find out what is happening," the King began, "Marçhal Bergan, what did the box contain?"

Bergan took a deep breath and began, "The sorcerer was thankfully able to open the message box. Inside were multiple messages from an orc called Kradak, apparently the Overlord of their species. It seems that the Orcs are hiding in the Black Crater, within the Veiled Sea. They are preparing an attack on the rest of the world to get revenge for the Orcish War."

"Nonsense, the Orcs were wiped out at the end of the war," Captain Roskin spoke.

"It seems not," Bergan said, "The warriors and females fled their lands and have been hidden ever since. The necromancer that Sir Riswaell was sent to find was tasked with resurrecting the Orcs killed during the war to use in the invasion force. I doubt they will still need this army as they have made an alliance with the Gliss tribes. If they have been building their forces for the past seventy years then they will be a truly formidable foe. "

The whole room was silent, shocked by what they had heard, until the King stood from his chair.

"Well then, gentlemen, we have our work cut out for us. Sir Riswaell, spend the rest of the night in the palace, get some rest and I will have a new task for you in the morning. There is a spare room next to Prince Torvald's chambers. Everybody else, get some sleep. We shall meet again at first light. It seems that we are going to war."

Tarimev and Torvald will return in

The Heroes of Lotine: Rise of War

Printed in Great Britain
by Amazon